ANGEL FURY

By
J.E. Taylor

J.E. TAYLOR
SUPERNATURAL SUSPENSE
& DARK FANTASY AUTHOR

ANGEL FURY

Duty is a double-edged sword. It means putting yourself last, ripping you away from everyone you love while you complete an unreasonable quest just to keep them safe.

Tom Ryan left York. He left everything he loves to safeguard the last angel descendants.

Now he's back, still damned, still persecuted. Prophecy says York will burn, and everyone left who matters to Tom is in York. With no time to catch up and reconnect, Tom is thrust into a battle he's destined to lose.

There are only so many ways you can break a man before his wrath changes the status quo.

Rekindled by family, by love, by home and memories, the ruthless son of Ty Ryan steps into the shoes left under the family tree by his dad, and this time he's out of mercy.

Chapter 1

I TAKE A SEAT in the private airport in Greece and pull out the ragged map from the inside pocket of my equally worn leather jacket. Ten years ago, I set out to close all of Lucifer's portals around the world, and I've seen every corner of the planet in the process. My dog has been with me all this time, as well, and I stroke Sam's fur as she sits by my side, laying her head on my lap like she does after every long journey. It's as if she knows I'm damned tired.

I unfold the atlas, crossing off the last circle just outside of Athens and I send Sam an exhausted smile.

"It's done," I whisper and fold the remains of the map, tucking it back in my pocket. Her soft whine prompts me to rub her ears again. "Well, girl, I think it's time to go home."

Home.

The word seems foreign on my lips, especially since I really didn't think I'd live to set foot in York again. And trust me, there were times that doubt was warranted, and both Sam and I have the scars to prove it.

All told, I closed thirty-eight portals; some were easy, some not so much. I got in, scrubbed the land and got out. Most times, I didn't encounter resistance from anything, but when I did, it usually came in the form of a horde of demons or an equally undesirable foe.

But nothing was a match for my angel fire, especially when I thought Sam was in danger. Well, nothing except Lucifer. And that bastard only showed his face once. In Death Valley, of all places. Much to my chagrin, he kicked my ass and nearly killed Sam before I got my head in the game and let the angel fire rip. I rained it down with such force I left a crater behind.

Sam had been in bad shape, bloodied and broken, but at least she was still breathing when I carried her out of that crater. I hauled her close to ten miles across the desert. A normal healthy male would have plenty of issues carrying a seventy-pound German Shepherd that distance. It nearly killed me, between my blood loss, coupled with heat exhaustion, and a busted shoulder just to top it all off. The vet said it was a miracle she survived, and my doctors proclaimed the same about me.

Seeing her limp to my side again when I picked her up at the vet was well worth the six days in the hospital, followed by four months in a cast, followed by another six months in rehab, before I was given a clean bill to move on.

It was a valuable lesson.

I hadn't used my head. Instead, I operated on fury alone and lost the calculated advantage. I swore I wouldn't let that happen again. Unfortunately, I never got to test that theory.

A glance at the clock tells me I have a solid two and a half hours before someone from Ted Beaumont's organization lands to pick me up. I lean back in the chair, tucking my chin to my chest with Sam's leash hanging on my wrist. I close my eyes, drifting back over the years to the day I found Sam.

MY PHONE BUZZED YET again, like it had been for the past six hours, and I glanced at the caller ID. Bridget O'Keefe. Again. She wasn't going to let this go. I clenched my fists, fighting every instinct to answer. Instead, I glanced out the window of the little coffee shop in some rural nowhere in Ohio. The strip mall across the street had nothing of interest on my first scan, except maybe the miniscule animal shelter housed at the end.

Needing some sort of diversion to keep me from answering her calls, I threw money on the table, took one last sip of the coffee, and stepped outside. The road wasn't busy, so I crossed, taking my time to glance at some of the window displays on the storefronts. Anything to keep my brain occupied with something other than Bridget.

Last night I'd nearly turned around a dozen times, just thinking of her soft flesh under my hands, and the taste of her. I knew that memory would both drive me and bite me in the ass, but I didn't expect the fucking turmoil accosting me with every thought.

When I stepped into the shelter, my mind totally blocked Bridget out. The sheer chaos of the open space and playtime for the dogs had my focus. I gave a nod to one of the shelter workers and she bounced over with a smile.

"Hi. My name is Nikolina. How may I help you?"

I returned her smile and just watched the dogs playing. I turned my gaze to hers, and, on impulse, asked, "You wouldn't happen to have any German Shepherd puppies, would you?"

The blues and greens in her aura flared at the question, as did the light in her eyes. "You're in luck! We had a litter delivered today. Come with me," she said, and led me to the rear section of the shelter and a smaller play area with bumbling pups.

I squatted and waited. My eyes studied each puppy until they fell on her. Sam was sitting on the opposite side, staring at me. When our eyes met, she trotted through the pack to the spot right in front of me, where she sat and waited just as patiently as I had. It was eerie and felt right as rain.

"I want this one." I pointed and looked up at the salesgirl.

Her eyebrows were already arched, and then her gaze moved from the little puppy to me.

"That's the damnedest thing I think I've ever seen." She nodded as she spoke, and I couldn't help but smile.

"Dogs choose their owners. Not the other way around," I said and scooped the puppy up into my arms, following her to the front.

She pulled out paperwork for adoption and slid it across the counter for me to fill out. I scribble the information while the puppy licked my face. I laughed and dodged her tongue, but for some reason, I didn't want to put her down, either, for fear someone else would step inside and steal her from me before I could finish the paperwork.

"You really are lucky. We don't normally get them this young. Usually the dogs are older, and the owners just don't want them anymore." She glanced over her shoulder at the dogs playing together. "At least they seem to get along, but sometimes we get one or two that have to stay in their kennels during playtime." She smiled at me. "I'm sure these puppies will go fast. It's unfortunate, but the owner passed away and their family had no idea what to do with these little rascals." She kept chattering on and I finally pushed the paper across the counter.

"I guess I need supplies as well," I said and glanced around at my limited options.

"I can hook you up with a collar and leash, but for anything else, I'd suggest Petsmart, which is only a mile down the road," she whispered over the counter.

I gave her a nod, she found a small red collar and a light leash, and I passed her the shelter fee along with another twenty-five bucks for the supplies.

With the leash on, I gently put Sam on the ground and started out of the store.

"Good luck!" Nikolina yelled after me and I gave her a wave before I walked back to the crosswalk. Instead of letting Sam cross on her own, I scooped her up and jogged to my car.

The minute I got her within the confines of the car, she sat and just stared at me as if I was supposed to impart some ancient wisdom or something.

"I hope you don't mind me calling you Sam," I said. Her tail wagged, and she stood, letting out this pitiful puppy yelp that immediately formed a grin on my face. I pulled my phone out and snapped a picture of her. "You just sit down and stay right there until we get to Petsmart. Then you can show me all the things you want. Okay, girl?"

Again, the wag of her tail and a bark followed.

I searched for the store, and just as the GPS loaded, a text flashed on my screen.

Fuck you, Ryan.

Bridget's use of my last name told me just how pissed she was, which was better than having her a crying mess. I debated on answering, but starting a dialog would only string her along and give her hope where there might be nothing but heartache for her.

The dog crawled across the console and onto my lap, as if she knew I needed reinforcement of some sort, and I glance beyond the phone in my hand at her. She lay her head on my thigh and gave the biggest sigh I've ever heard from a puppy.

I popped the phone on the console plug and moved her to the passenger seat before I put the car in gear and headed to find dog supplies.

"MR. RYAN?" A VOICE cuts through the memory, and I open my eyes, glancing at the pilot approaching me.

I stand and study him for a moment. Ten years flood back, along with the unwelcome sorrow. "Josh," I say, as his name pops into my head. I stick out my hand to the pilot who had flown me home from this precise airport the night my daughter died.

He hesitates and then clasps my hand. His memory flashes in my head and I drop my hand after a quick shake.

Sam whines at my side, as if she can feel the cracking of my reinforced heart.

"This is my dog, Sam." I lay my hand on her head, reassuring her I am okay. It has been long enough that I don't curl into a tight ball, fighting the pain through tear-stained vision anymore, but she remembers, just as well as I do.

"Ted said there will be a car for you in Wolfeboro," he says and reaches for my bag on the seat. This time, I let him carry my cargo onto the plane. "Unfortunately..."

"You don't have a flight crew," I finish his thought.

He lets out a soft chuckle. "And I'm getting near the max flying within twenty-four hours."

"I can help fly if you need a co-pilot," I say, and his eyebrows rise. "I had a bit of time to kill when I was laid up in California and figured a pilot's license might come in handy." I pull out my wallet and show him my certificate.

"I might take you up on that," he says, but his mind is shadowed with doubt, especially with the memory of my mental state being so fractured the last time he flew me home from Greece.

I don't respond. I just follow him with Sam at my heels.

The flight home takes much longer than that first trek, but I'm not using my powers to make this sucker fly at some insane mach speed like last time, either. Sam is the perfect traveling companion, calm and serene, and as always, has her head in my lap.

The hum of the airplane drops my eyelids farther and farther until the shadows mix together.

Chapter 2

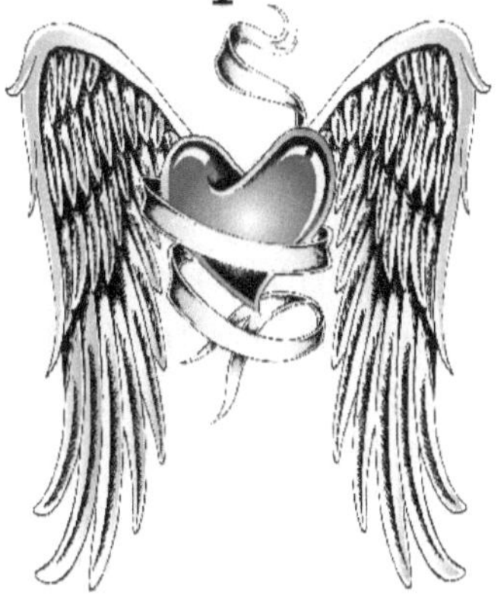

THE BUMP OF TIRES on pavement jerks me out of sleep and I rub my eyes, pushing myself up from the arm of the chair. Sam jumps off the seat and stretches, yawning in the process, and I follow suit.

Josh comes out of the cockpit looking haggard and exhausted, and I give him a nod of thanks.

"I didn't want to wake you," he says and waves towards the seat where I fell asleep.

"I appreciate it." I am still groggy, but I don't think I've slept that soundly since I was a teenager. When Josh reaches for my bag, I say, "I've got this. You look like you need some rest."

I exchange a handshake and climb down the stairs into the cool spring New Hampshire air. Sam follows and I open the hangar door for her, letting her lead the way.

"Mr. Ryan?" a chauffeur stands, folding the paper he had been reading.

"Yes, sir," I reply, and head towards him with Sam and my light load.

"Mr. Beaumont said I should take you anywhere you want to go."

I smile my appreciation. Being as foggy as I am, I probably will make a better passenger than a driver.

"I need to make a stop in Brooksfield, and then I'll want to head to York."

"Sure thing," he says and glances at my dog. "She's a beauty," he adds.

"Thanks. I'll have to find a grassy spot for her before we go."

He opens the door for me, and I glance at the small parking area and a large grass patch on the opposite side of the asphalt. I unhook Sam and she waits.

"Go on, girl."

She takes off straight for that grass and her sniff-circle-sniff-pee routine ensues. The relief in her features is actually readable and I smile at her, waiting. As soon as she is back, we climb into the back of the town car.

From Wolfeboro, it's less than a half hour south to Brooksfield and I give him the address to Steve's cottage on Mirror Lake where Paradise Cove resides. My hand passes over the map in my breast pocket and I close my eyes, saying a brief prayer that it's enough. I'm done with being a nomad with little to no connection with those I care about. I want to plant roots and let Sam live out her days chasing balls in the surf.

When we pull into the long dirt driveway, I have a moment to wonder if Steve and Jennifer are at the cottage, but as we round the last bend, the darkened windows and empty driveway indicate no one is home. The driver pulls to a stop and puts the car in park.

"Wait here, I shouldn't be long," I say as I slip out of the back seat. Sam climbs out with me and I cross the dark lawn, smiling at the crunch of the grass under my feet. I don't hesitate, like I had that night ten years ago. Instead, I tromp through the path in the woods until I'm standing on the soft green moss underfoot.

Nothing has changed. Nothing ever changes in the cove. Even in the dead of winter, flowers poke from the edges of the snow, creating a surreal landscape. Now that the winter snows have melted, the flowers bloom vibrant, even in the dark, creating a luminous glow like that of a nightlight.

I pull out the map and clear my throat, not sure of whose name to call. Eventually, I look up.

"Mom?" My voice sounds meek, like a scolded child's voice, and Sam whines and leans her entire body against my leg. I shift, disgusted with how weak I sound. I'm almost forty, for God's sake; I shouldn't sound like a scared little kid.

By the end of my mental rant, I realize there has been no answer.

I repeat her name a little louder and my question echoes out onto the lake.

Still no answer.

"I did what was asked." I hold up the map as if the heavens could see it.

"Mom? Dad?" I call, because the silence is deafening. Sam nudges me again, her ears falling back on her head as she reads my budding distress correctly.

"God damn it! Answer me!" This time my voice bellows with a growl.

Nothing. No ripple of the air, no smoke, no heavenly light, and I'm left in the dark.

"Raven!" I scream, the anger getting the best of me, I can feel it building under my skin, the burn of it right there in my simmering blood.

This time, the air changes and the form standing in the middle of the cove, doesn't settle my nerves. As a matter of fact, I'm much more on guard than if it was a member of my family.

The archangel Michael walks towards me, and his face is a mask of wrath.

"You dare step onto this sacred ground?"

"I closed all the goddamned portals," I wave the map at him, but take a step back, wary of the archangel. I not only harbored Lucifer's grace, but in killing Damian, I also absorbed Gabriel's and Michael's grace.

So, I am as much a target to Michael as I am to Lucifer. I shift, setting myself in a defensive position, protecting my chest at all costs.

Sam's low growl causes me to look away from the angry angel and down at her.

Her teeth are bared, and all the hair on her neck stands on end.

"Sit," I command and her growl fades as she glances up at me in confusion. "I know he's dangerous," I whisper and look up at Michael, weighing my chances. He no longer sports wings and his power is not as strong as it once was, but he could do the same type of damage that Lucifer did to Sam and me back in Death Valley, especially since this is Michael's home turf.

Paradise Cove is a portal to heaven. And based on the reception, it looks like I'm still not welcome.

"I closed the portals. Every last one of them," I say and throw the map in his direction.

"We are very well aware of what you have done."

The venom in his tone catches me off guard. I'm at a loss and I just stare.

His eyes narrow and he crosses his arms. "You really have no idea, do you?"

"Apparently not," I say. "I kind of expected a thank you," I add, pointing at the faded map lying at Michael's feet.

His sardonic laugh echoes. "You really are an inept fool." He scoops up the map and scans all my red marks for the closed portals.

"I worked my ass off to close every goddamned portal on that list!" Anger brews beyond a simmer and the heat spreads. "I spent the last ten years doing CJ's job, and this is the thanks I get?"

He glares at me and tosses the paper back.

I catch it before it hits my chest.

"You closed the portals, but you left Lucifer topside," he growls and takes a step towards me.

Like a flash, Sam is between us and her menacing growl fills the space.

My anger dulls and I blink, trying to reconcile my achievements with what he just stated.

"I closed the portals," I say again, but with less force.

"Yes, and you locked Lucifer out of hell, you stupid bastard!"

The map crumples in my hand, and I glared at Michael. "How the hell was I supposed to know that? Huh?" I step closer with purpose, crowding Sam between us. "I was told to close the portals, and I did. And now you're insulting me?"

The burn rakes my skin and from the widening of Michael's eyes, I know I've transformed. His shock is momentary, and then his growl of anger forming Lucifer's name announces his intentions. He charges and I sidestep my dog, parrying into a block before I toss Michael over my hip and he slams into the ground on his back.

"I am not Lucifer," I yell in his face and step back, calming the burn. I know I look exactly like that murdering bastard when I lose my temper, but I am not the devil. I take another step, and another breath, putting more distance between us. "And I don't understand. I did what was asked of me. Why are you so pissed off?"

Michael sits up slowly, still staring me down. "Give me my grace," he orders.

I know from CJ how to transfer grace, but I hesitate and shake my head. I had other plans for the magic inside me, plans that would ensure the safety of my nephew and Damian's daughter. "No. I'm saving that for my nephew," I say. "I have a feeling he might need it more than either you or I."

The anger burning in Michael softens and his head cocks. "You... care about his welfare?"

"Why the fuck do you think I've been running all over the world? It certainly isn't to enjoy the perks of travel."

"I didn't think you gave a damn about anyone but yourself, especially after what you did to Damian," he snaps.

"I thought I could save my daughter." I glance out at the water for a minute before looking back at Michael. "I screwed that up royally." I step closer and offer him my hand.

Michael stares at it and then meets my gaze again. He takes my grip and the instant he is on his feet; his hand forms a claw and covers my heart, his fingers dig into my flesh with purpose.

My reaction is immediate, and the explosion moves outwards from the center of my being, knocking him back into the woods beyond the edge of the cove. I can't pull the power back in. It's already formed a life of its own and it engulfs the cove in flame, like it has every other portal on the planet, obliterating it off the map.

I turn, scooping up Sam before she is consumed, bolting towards the path. My heart thunders in my ears as the voices of my family echo in my head in one final chorus of "Don't!" Then the door slams, shutting off any further contact with the dead.

I trip on a root, and Sam goes flying. She lands on her feet, and I find myself on my hands and knees, horrified at what just transpired.

I roll and scan the crop circle that is left. All the beauty and lushness of the cove is gone and only dirt remains. Michael slowly stands in the protection of the woods a few feet beyond my destruction.

Holy fuck.

My chest clenches with the knowledge that I've just locked Michael out of heaven.

Chapter 3

THE DRIVER KEEPS LOOKING at me in the rearview mirror, as if I've lost it completely.

I can't blame him. I came skidding back nearly throwing myself in the car yelling for him to go, to drive, to get the hell out of dodge—right now.

I think we were moving even before I got the door closed, leaving a path of dust and dirt.

Sam pants next to me and I turn just in time to catch Michael stepping on the lawn. Even with the building distance, I gulp at the glare in his eyes. He's coming after me.

In resignation, I lay my head against the seat, going over my options. I'm not sure if CJ will back me up on this. Not when I've closed his only contact with our parents. I run my hand over my face and lean forward.

"Instead of the address on Roaring Rock, please take me to 375 River Road."

"Yes, sir." He glances at me again with a nod.

I calm my raw nerves by stroking Sam's head. She huffs that heavy sigh like she did that first day, and I give her a gentle pat before continuing the calming stroke, from between her ears down to below her collar.

Lucifer's on the loose.

That thought keeps pinging into my consciousness, bringing with it a fear that my coming home might put those I love in the crosshairs between two angry angels. The dark scenery passes, and I catch my reflection in the window every time a streetlight passes. My stubble has transitioned to scruff over the last few days, and my hair is almost as long as it was when I left ten years ago. The lines at the corner of my eyes are more pronounced, but outside of those faint crow's feet, I look the same as I did the day I picked up Sam from that animal shelter.

When we pull into the driveway, a car is parked in the carport, but the house is dark, like it should be at two in the morning. The agency name catches my attention and I pause, staring at it over the top of the car. Ryan-O'Keefe. At least she kept my name on the marquis.

I shook my head to focus and leaned into the car, grabbing the end of Sam's leash along with my backpack before handing the driver a sizeable tip for driving me all over creation.

With Sam in tow, I cross to the front door. I no longer have keys, so I close my eyes, disengaging the locks. Stepping inside feels a little like I am trespassing, and as soon as I latch and lock the door behind me, I turn back to what used to be the reception area.

Shock fills every cell. The old entry, along with what used to be my office, is open and decorated like a living area and not an office. The door to Damian's office is still intact and I debate on which direction to go.

The comfortable-looking couch won the coin toss in my head, and I cross, setting my bag down, and fall onto the soft fabric. Sam stretched out on the floor next to me. She really didn't have a choice, either. I am not going to let her snoop around the rest of the house and scare the bejesus out of Bridget.

I close my eyes hoping to catch a few hours of sleep before I'm thrown to the curb.

A PIERCING SCREAM SLAYS my dream, bolting me into a sitting position. My hand instinctively tightens, grasping the leash before Sam lunges at whatever vibrated my eardrums to the point of pain.

A very pretty, blonde girl with wide blue eyes is frozen in place as much as I am. I expected Bridget to find me here, not a girl who could be...

My eyes widen as Bridget slides into place next to the screaming girl. A pistol is trained in my direction, in hands that shake from pure adrenaline. My gaze jumps between Bridget and the girl next to her, and the relation is clear. I am looking at Bridget's daughter.

The gun is slowly lowered as recognition sets in. "Tom?"

It's the girl's turn to level a surprised look in Bridget's direction. "You know him?" she balks and waves in my direction.

"Yes. From a long time ago," she says to her daughter. "April, this is Tom Ryan. Tom, my daughter April."

"Ryan, as in the name on the sign?"

Bridget nods. "Go. You'll be late for the bus," she says and points towards the door.

April gives me a wary look and then disappears. The door opens and closes a moment later and I stare at Bridget.

"This is Sam," I say, remembering I have a dog attached to my arm.

Bridget doesn't even look. "What the fuck are you doing in my house?" She flips the safety on her gun and crosses the room, dropping it on the coffee table as she passes by. Bridget stands with her back to me, waiting until the bus pulls away with April safely on board.

"Well?" she asks as she turns and levels a frosty glare in my direction.

"I finished closing the portals."

"Big fucking deal."

Sam whines and paws my leg, her sign that she needs to go out.

"I'll be right back," I say and get an eye roll in return. I let Sam out and stand at the door, watching while she does her business. A low whistle calls her back inside and I return to the couch, unsure if I should sit down or just go, and while it would be easy to dive into her mind to find out the answers to the questions swirling in my head, I leave well enough alone.

She would probably pop a cap in my ass if she caught me snooping in her head.

I gave her a small smile. "I'm sorry I hurt you," I say in barely a whisper.

She moves across the room and stops in front of me before she shoves me with everything she has. I stumble back a step and Sam growls. I give my dog the hand signal for stay, but that doesn't stop the menacing rumble coming from her.

"You're sorry?" Her voice is feral along with the anger boiling in her eyes. "You left and didn't even bother to answer any of my calls or texts. I didn't know if you were alive or dead."

The next time she goes to shove me I grab her wrists.

"I screwed up. With you, with everything," I say to soften her anger. Now that our skin is touching, the emotional turmoil pounding in her chest travels into me just as acutely. Her aura flares with it. "And if I picked up the phone and heard your voice, I would have turned my ass around."

She tries to break free of my grip, but I keep hold, making her meet my eyes.

"Let go," she says through clenched teeth.

I drop my hands away.

"Why are you here?" she asks again, but this time there's less bite to the question.

"I didn't know where else to go," I say and look around with a shrug. "This is the closest thing I've got to home." I look at her when I speak.

"This is my home. You need to go book a hotel, because you cannot stay here."

I give a nod and sigh. "I gather you're married now?" I hook my thumb towards the door where her daughter went.

Bridget hesitates looking beyond me and back. She shakes her head and laughs, looking at the ceiling. "No, Tom. I never got married."

I raise my eyebrows as a dawning idea blooms. "How old is she?"

"She turns ten in July."

My brain runs the calculation and I glance towards the door again. That's when it strikes me. Her daughter's aura was bright. Bright enough to indicate angel blood, and my gaze snaps to Bridget's.

I stumble into the nearest seat, just gawking at her.

"The answer to your question is yes. She's yours, but you have no right to be in our lives, not after abandoning us for so long."

I'm too stunned to speak. That familiar numbness takes over, as if all my synapses cannot handle the emotional swirl in my stomach and I run my hands into my hair, lowering my elbows to my knees.

"I fucked up again," I say quietly, and the full scope of what this means hits like a bulldozer. "Lucifer is locked topside." I look up at Bridget. "And so is Michael."

"Michael who?" Her arms cross.

I lean back. "The archangel. And both of them want to kick my ass."

"They'll have to get in line," she says.

I rise to my feet and cross, stopping in front of her. "Bri..."

"You don't get to call me that!" Her outburst is followed by the sting of her hand on my cheek. Sam growls in response, but I keep Bridget's angry gaze.

There's only one way to make her understand and I grab her face in my palms, pressing my lips to hers before she can react. She struggles, but I push the past ten years into her mind and at the same time siphon her memories. Her struggles cease and she opens her mouth to tell me to stop, but the moment our tongues intertwine, her hands slide up my chest. The warmth of her surrounds me, but it's only temporary. When I pull away, tears swim in her eyes, and she pushes off me, distancing herself.

"You can't do that," she whispers, and her voice shakes. "You can't fuck with my head like that."

"Bri," I whisper. "You kept me alive, just as much as Sam did."

"Don't," she points at me.

"I'm sorry, but I left to keep you safe."

"Bullshit! You didn't do it for me. You did it for you."

I look beyond her out the window, analyzing her accusation. "You're right. I did it so I wouldn't have to see you murdered at the hands of Lucifer."

Sam nudges my hand and whines. I point to the floor. "Lie down," I say, meeting my dog's worried stare. "I'm okay, just lie down." I clarify when she doesn't move.

She lowers to the floor, keeping her eyes on me.

"I did it so I wouldn't be put in the position of sacrificing myself for you." Admitting the selfishness of my actions is humbling, and I slide my hands in my pockets, letting out a soft laugh as I study the floor. "Because that's what I would have done if he got hold of you. I would have let him rip my heart out, because it wouldn't matter anymore."

I look up, meeting her skeptical gaze and throw a shrug her way.

"You are so full of shit." She remains planted in place.

She had my memories. She knew I wasn't bullshitting her, but I also knew the depth of how hurt she was. I'd crushed her spirit when I left. She opened up to me that night, letting me see her deepest fears, her darkest times, and I slipped away in the dead of night with only a few words scribbled on paper as an explanation. I took the coward's way out.

"I still care, Bri." She shakes her head at my admission and instead of arguing with her, I look around at the modifications to the house bathed in daylight. "I like what you've done to my office," I say, avoiding her stark stare.

"Tom, you can't stay here," she says. "I can't have you anywhere near April."

I close my eyes and nod, and the emptiness creeps back in, but I understand. Affiliating with me is a death sentence, at least while Lucifer walks the earth. "Okay."

I turn to leave, picking up my bag.

"Tom," she whispers, and I glance over my shoulder at her. "I stopped caring a while ago."

I huff a laugh. "You're as bad a liar as I am." I don't wait for a response, instead I snap my fingers and Sam is at my side. I cross the threshold into the cool morning air with no clue of where to go next.

Chapter 4

I STAND AT THE front door of the house I grew up in and glance down at Sam standing at my side. I have no idea how welcomed I'll be, or not, and I raise my hand to knock. The door opens before my knuckles hit the wood.

My brother, CJ Ryan, stands on the other side, with that mischievous sparkle in his eye. He hasn't changed one bit since I left, and that old flare of envy blooms.

"Val and I took bets as to how long you'd stand out here," CJ says, and he breaks into a broad smile, pulling me into a hug.

I return the welcome. "You might not be so happy to see me after we talk," I say as the hug breaks.

His smile falters, but the moment his gaze drops to my side, it's back.

"Who's this?" he asks, crouching.

"Sam. She's been with me since before I got to Detroit."

CJ looks up with a smile. "Good choice in names," he says and puts his hand out.

Sam tentatively takes a sniff and then allows CJ to pet her. Valerie stands, leaning on the doorjamb to the kitchen, and she gives me a nod of acknowledgement. But there is something just below the surface. A warning of sorts.

"He's here, isn't he?"

CJ stands and sighs. "Yes."

I close my eyes and hang my head, shaking it slowly before I meet my brother's gaze. "And you're still happy to see me?"

"Hell, yes, I'm happy to see you. You're my brother and I haven't seen you or talked to you outside a random text in ten years. I missed you, bro," he says and the sincerity in his eyes and the purity of his aura tell me all I needed to know. "Don't just stand there, get your ass in here," he says, yanking me inside.

I step inside, dropping my bag on the floor. "You have a couple of bowls so I can feed Sam?"

"Sure," Valerie says, and turns away into the kitchen.

I unzip my duffel bag and pull out the dog food, bringing it with me to the kitchen. I slow to a stop halfway to where Valerie has two bowls in her hand. Three kids sit at the breakfast nook with workbooks open in front of them. A boy and two girls. The boy is readily identifiable. He's CJ's doppelgänger, much like CJ was our father's.

The girls are a few years younger, but all three kids have the same features and the bright, almost blinding auras.

"You had twins?" My gaze snaps to CJ, and he smiles.

"Kids, say hi to your Uncle Tom," CJ says as I take the bowls from Valerie. "Tom, this is Alex, Amber and Arianna."

"Hi," I say and pour a bowl full of dog food. "This is Sam." I add water to the second bowl and set it on the floor before standing and facing them.

I get the smiles and hellos of children trying to be polite, and a pang hits. I should have been around to see them grow up. Instead, I was running around the world closing portals.

Beyond the children, sitting on the couch, is Michael and the glare he sends in my direction makes me stay close to Sam, where I feel reasonably safe.

"He will not harm you," CJ says quietly, so only I can hear.

I huff and meet my brother's gaze. "I think you might underestimate just how pissed he is at me."

"Come on," CJ says to me and heads for the door at the opposite side of the kitchen, leading to the finished basement.

I glance at the group, send a strained smile, and follow my brother downstairs. The playscape I remember gave way to a sectional and gaming controls and an arts and craft table in the corner.

CJ takes a seat, studying me, and now that we were alone, his smile has disappeared. I take the cushion opposite him.

"Before you say anything, I need to thank you. You gave up a hell of a lot to go out there and do my job for me. I can't begin to repay you."

"But I fucked it all up," I say.

He laughs, shaking his head. "No. They fucked it up by not telling us all this shit." He points at the ceiling, and I catch the burning anger underneath his calm exterior. "They told me I had to close the portals and they never once said to make sure

Lucifer was there when I closed the last one. I shut Michael down on that. Yes, he's pissed, but it's not your fault."

I stare at CJ and press my lips together. "He didn't tell you he's locked here, too, did he?"

CJ blinks and leans back in the seat. The confusion written in his features tells me he does not have the full story.

I choose my words carefully. "Michael tried to... steal the grace inside me."

The clarity of what that means slams home in CJ and his jaw tightens.

"I lost control," I add with a shrug. "Paradise Cove is no more."

He's still reeling from my confession when I add. "Did you know I'm a father?"

His entire form sinks into the cushions and CJ rubs his face, collecting his thoughts.

"I didn't know about Paradise Cove," he finally says, and meets my gaze.

My muscles tighten, and I close my eyes at the burn. "And you didn't think to tell me I had another daughter?"

"Would it have made a difference?" He crosses his arms and sends me that challenging raise of his eyebrow.

I bite down on the automatic yes that wants to come out, because it's as much of a lie as Bridget telling me she no longer cares. Finally, I shake my head because if I had known, it would not have changed my course.

"I figured, why give you something else to kick yourself over."

While it irks me, I understand CJ's rationale. The jangle of Sam's collar pulls our attention to the stairwell, and she comes trotting over, settling at my feet.

CJ smiles. "What possessed you to get a dog?"

I shrug and lean down, running my hand over her soft fur. "I figured I needed something to keep me from becoming suicidal." I meet CJ's gaze. "It probably was a good call; otherwise, I would have died in Death Valley."

CJ cocked his head. "The crater?"

I chuckled. "Yeah. That was the only time Lucifer appeared. Instead of using my head, I had no strategy and no control over the emotional turmoil, and he nearly killed both of us."

Sam shifts to a sitting position and lays her head on my knee. I scratch behind her ears. Her tail slowly sways in contentment.

"I carried her ten miles to the nearest town and then spent the next year in physical therapy."

CJ's eyes widened. "And you didn't think to call us?"

"Oh, I thought of it. Every time I had to figure out how to put clothes on with my shoulder in a fucking cast, but I sucked it up. I had a lot of time to kill and some serious therapy to get back into fighting shape. Instead of just wallowing in my pain, I used the time and enrolled in a flight course."

"Really?" CJ asks, but he isn't mocking me, he's impressed.

"Yep. I earned a private pilot's license." It's something I'm proud of, and it's something my brother doesn't have.

"So, when are you buying a plane?"

I laugh. It would be like CJ to ask that question, and we both have that kind of money to spare, but I hadn't considered buying a plane, not when I have Ted Beaumont's private jet company on speed dial. "I haven't put much thought into that," I answer.

"You should. Think of all the exotic places you can take Bridget whenever you want to." He grins and sends a wink my way.

"I can go anywhere right now; all I have to do is pick up the phone. And as far as Bridget is concerned, she's still pissed at me," I say, and CJ laughs.

"Yes. I hear about how much of an asshole you are every time she's here. But don't let that discourage you. Underneath all that spitfire, she is still in love with you. The question is, do you feel the same?"

"I don't know. It's been ten years."

His eyes narrow and I feel the tickle in my mind.

"Bullshit. She's been on your mind almost the entire time you were gone."

"It's a moot point. She wants nothing to do with me and she certainly doesn't want me anywhere near April until after the threat is gone. I don't blame her, either. Seems I'm a walking death sentence, or hadn't you noticed?"

"Cut the pity party shit." CJ leans forward in the seat. "You didn't screw up by leaving to do what you needed to. That's something that, while hard to digest, is forgivable. Where you did screw up was excommunicating yourself from all of us." He takes a deep breath. "Both Valerie and I get it. We've been casualties of Lucifer's before, and know what kind of focus it takes to commit to the quest you were given by default. It should have been me out there, but I couldn't leave my family, especially after what happened to yours."

"CJ, he's coming for us. You know that, right?"

CJ nods and glances down at the floor. "Yes, I know that. I have two daughters that are on his acquisition list." He snaps his gaze to mine and there is an underlying controlled fury there. "And he's been powering up for the confrontation."

"He's been killing angel blood again?"

"Yes, and he's obliterated the list."

I can't help my jaw from falling open. There had been hundreds of names on that list, but considering I hadn't had a run in with him for almost eight years, perhaps I should have been able to make that educated guess. "Is that why Paige and Austin are here in York?"

CJ gives me a nod. "If you hadn't been such a stubborn jackass, and had returned my calls, you would know all this."

I concentrate on petting Sam for a few minutes, trying to calm the nerves bundling in my stomach. CJ's reproach is not without credence. He has every right to be as pissed as Bridget is.

"I'm not," CJ says quietly, pulling my gaze to his. "I am just glad you're back. For purely selfish reasons, of course," he smiles.

"Yeah, you don't want to be the only one tasked with everyone's safety."

His smile deepens and he shrugs. "It's been tough. There isn't anyone else who can do it besides you."

I study him, reading into his words. "None of your kids..." I can't finish the sentence. I naturally assumed they'd inherited his gifts, but the slow shake of his head unnerves me. It means that he and I are the only ones with the ability to stand up against Lucifer.

"If we fail..." He stops, keeping eye contact.

"It means the end of times." My words produce a shiver in both of us.

Chapter 5

"GUYS?" VALERIE'S VOICE CALLS down the stairs. I glance at my watch. CJ and I have been shooting the shit for hours.

"Yeah, hun?"

"I need you on grill duty." Valerie pokes her head around the stairwell corner.

"Sure thing," CJ says, getting to his feet.

"I naturally assumed you were staying for dinner," she says to me as we approach the stairs. "I also assumed you might need a place to stay tonight, so I made the bed in the guest room."

"Thanks," I say, and offer her a strained smile.

CJ passes her and heads upstairs, with Sam on his heels, but Valerie stops me with a hand on my arm. She glances over her shoulder to make sure CJ is out of hearing range, and then she brings her hard stare back to mine.

"You and I need to get something straight."

"What's that?" I ask, thinking she was going to tell me I was not welcome in her home after everything I have done.

"You don't ever skip town without talking with your brother, you hear me?"

I blink at her and raise my eyebrows.

"You may be fine on your own, but CJ was a fucking mess, and I'm not dealing with that again, you understand?"

I just nod.

"And you'd better get shit straightened out with Bridget." Her finger pokes my chest.

"I thought..."

Her glare shuts me up. "I was angry at first. Raven was my best friend. I shouldn't have judged you, but I did. I thought you were being a self-centered jackass." She shrugs. "But after you left, I got to know Bridget a little better, and I think Raven would approve."

"Oh." I'm not sure what else to say and her gaze softens. She pulls me into a hug.

"It's good to have you back," she whispers and steps away, heading upstairs, leaving me humbled.

Sam sticks her head around the corner and just stares at me.

"I'm coming," I mutter, and climb the stairs. I need a second to put on a smile and cheery disposition for the kids. When I step into the kitchen, I scan the family room. "Where did Michael go?"

"I asked him to go visit with Naomi," Valerie says, and CJ's dimples deepened, but he kept his mouth shut.

"Didn't want a moody archangel hanging out with the kids?" I say what CJ wouldn't, and Valerie presses her lips together against a smile.

"If that guy was an archangel, where're his wings?" Alex asks and looks up from the papers spread on the counter.

"It's a long story, Alex. Finish up your homework." Valerie taps the counter. The girls have already moved to the couch and are engaged in some kid's television program.

Valerie turns to me. "You have still not learned to self-regulate what comes out of your mouth." Valerie's tone is scolding, but she's laughing at the same time.

"Guess not," I say, and heat fills my cheeks. "Can I help with anything?" I ask, waving at the food prep on the kitchen counters, while CJ grabs the plate of burgers and heads out into the backyard.

"I'm almost done, but if you want to set the table, you can."

"Sure," I say, and cross to where the silverware drawer had been in the old house. I find a utensil drawer instead.

"Over here," she says, and points to the drawer on the inside of the breakfast bar.

"Thanks." I gather the appropriate number of forks, knives and spoons for six of us. "The dining room table?" I ask, pointing to the front portion of the family room where the table sits.

"Sure," she says and continues to build an appealing salad.

I set the table and then slide onto one of the bar stools at the breakfast nook, next to my nephew. "How's Naomi," I ask, finally voicing the question I dreaded asking.

Valerie meets my gaze and before she answers, she glances at Alex sitting next to me and I get that this conversation is best reserved for after the kids are in bed. "She's good."

I glance at the papers Alex has strewn over the counter and recognize my brother's blocked script. With just a raise of an eyebrow, Valerie answers my question with two words.

"Home schooled."

"Really?"

"That common core crap is making the kids stupid," she says, and I let out a laugh. "My kids are already reading at a high school level, and Alex is doing advanced math. They wouldn't be doing that in the public grade schools," she adds, and I catch pride radiating from her.

"Well, they are CJ's kids," I say and she gives me that look again. "No offense. I know you're smart, but he's a genius. Seems logical his kids would excel in the same way."

"Dad's a genius?" Alex asks looking between us.

"He didn't tell you that?" I meet his inquisitive stare. "Your dad qualifies as Mensa, just like your grandfather did."

Alex glances at her mother and she nods.

"CJ has a pretty tough curriculum, too," she smiles. "Naomi's kids had some... challenges with it and they went to York High last year instead of sticking with CJ."

"Huh." I can't help the grunt. It seems to me, Naomi would have a difficult time letting her kids out of her sight, but I keep my narrative quiet.

"Naomi volunteers at the school," Valerie says, catching my thoughts.

Sometimes the mind reading ability we share is a good thing and I smile at her with a nod.

"I think I'll go help your father on the grill." I slide off the chair and head out to the patio, letting Sam accompany me. The ocean breeze is more than welcome, and for the first time in over ten years, I feel like I'm home.

"You doing okay?" CJ asks as he glances at me.

I stare at the familiar rock wall and the ocean beyond, and nod. "Yeah. At least for the moment." We both watch Sam sniff the property, do her business in the far corner garden, and trot back, like she'd just delivered a package of gold.

"I'll clean that up," I nod toward the corner.

"At least she went in the garden. Remember cleaning up the landmines all over the yard with Dad's dog?"

"Yeah, and it sucked when we missed some. Inevitably, someone would land in it when we played football here."

CJ belts out a laugh. "You remember that time when Bear slid right through a patch of crap? He was covered in it."

My laughter joins him at the memory. That was long before our senior year, when everything went to hell. It's one of my fonder high school memories and the entire team had ended on the ground laughing while Bear stomped around covered in German Shepherd shit and swearing at the top of his lungs.

"He had to have been a shit magnet," I laugh, because if memory serves me correctly, he was usually the one who found the missed piles in our yard.

CJ glances at the slider, still laughing. "You gotta watch the language, okay?" he asks once he winds down.

"Sure." It's been forever since I had little ears around, and I'll have to attempt to keep my language clean.

CJ opens the grill and flips the burgers one last time, laying cheese slices on all but one. He closes the top and glances at me with a smile. A few seconds later, he opens the top and transfers the meat from the grill irons to the plate.

The minute the sliders open, the kids run to the table, where Valerie has already garnished the plates with salad and French fries. CJ flips the burgers onto the waiting rolls and we all take a seat. I don't remember the last time I had a home grilled burger, and as I sink my teeth through the juicy meat, I close my eyes.

"This is the best damned burger I think I've ever had," I mumble around the bite glancing between CJ and Valerie. They both smile at me and between both of them, I hear "language," in my head. "Pardon my language, kids, it's just I haven't had a real hamburger in years."

Their eyes grow as big as saucers.

"I've been all over the world, and I can honestly say, I missed this." I focus on eating the rest of the meal on my plate, while what I assume is normal dinner chatter resumes. It's more of a drill on what the kids learned today before the conversation transitions to tomorrow and Valerie's work schedule.

"How long are you staying?" one of the girls asks, and I can't remember which one she is.

"Just a couple of days until I can find a place," I say.

CJ's eyebrow rises. "You can stay as long as you'd like. We've got enough room."

Instead of thanking him for the offer, I turn to Valerie, because it's really in her court. My brother would offer me a place to stay if they lived in a one-room shack. I don't want to impose, but I hadn't really thought through living arrangements at all when I decided to come home.

I no longer have a house of my own in York. I never stayed around to see the final rebuild of the house on Nubble Road, and when Austin texted to ask if I knew of any decent rental properties, I offered a rent-to-own contract on the house. They are more than halfway through the contract now.

I had figured the couch in my office was my best bet for the time being, but Bridget made it perfectly clear she didn't want me under that roof. Besides, my private office is gone, and that portion of the house acts as the living area for Bridget and her daughter.

I suppose I could see if my house on Lake Wentworth could be opened, but I really don't want to be that far away from the family, with everything I learned in the last twenty-four hours. So, it is either impose on CJ, or find a hotel.

She sends a soft smile in my direction. "CJ's right. You're welcome for as long as you'd like."

I look at the child who asked the question. "Do any of you mind if I stay here for a while?"

The girls emphatically shake their heads, their auras flared with welcoming golden light, and I sigh, glancing at the only one at the table who hasn't weighed in. Alex remains quiet as he picks at his food. I wait, even though I hear his internal dialog, weighing the options.

He finally raises his eyes to mine. "It's dangerous having you here, isn't it?"

"Alex," CJ snaps, and I put my hand up, silencing him.

"I got this," I say to my brother, before turning towards Alex. "Yes. It is. The reason I left when you were a baby was to protect you and your family. I thought I was doing that, but unfortunately, I didn't have all the facts, and may have made things worse for everyone." I glance around the table. "There are two furious archangels out there. You had the pleasure of meeting one today. He was the nice one, but I still think he wants to kick my a... butt." I correct my use of words at the last moment. "Michael won't hurt any of you," I add, to calm their growing fears.

"And the other one?" Alex asks.

I trade a glance with CJ.

"The other one isn't so nice." I say, watering down the truth to a palatable child's level. "So, yes. It is dangerous having me here."

"Why do they want to hurt you?" Amber asks from the other side of the table.

I inhale and slowly exhale. "Because your uncle stole something of theirs and they want it back."

Eyes all around the table widen and I wondered just how wide they would get if the kids knew I murdered my best friend to steal that something.

"Why don't you just give it back?"

I laugh a little. "I can't. It's kind of... inside me," I say.

"You could give Michael his back." Valerie's quiet comment pulls my attention to her.

"Really, we want to talk about this now?" CJ says, but neither Valerie nor I are paying attention.

He can help. Her silent communication echoes in my head.

He'll smite me the moment he has it back. I killed his nephew, and I'd do the same damned thing if I were in his shoes. I transmit, keeping her gaze.

Her color pales a fraction, and she trades a glance with CJ before addressing the kids. "Your Uncle Tom is kind of like Flynn Rider from Tangled."

"He's Eugene?" both Amber and Arianna say at the same time.

I can't help the smile that comes to my lips. That was one of Hannah's favorite movies, and we had seen it so many times that both Raven and I could drop quotes from the movie without so much as a blink. "I've never been compared to a Disney character before," I say, and Valerie smiles as well.

Even Alex is smiling. For a kid who's almost eleven, he certainly acts a hell of a lot older.

"If you stay, Sam stays, right?" Alex asks.

"Yes. Sam goes where I go."

He glances at my dog and then the rest of the family. "Then I guess I'm okay with it," he says.

"Well, then I guess I'm staying." I give him a pat on the back and stand, collecting the now empty plates.

"You're a guest," Valerie starts.

One glare from me, and she stops. "Let me at least feel like I'm earning my keep."

The slider opens when I'm halfway to the sink and I slow to a stop.

Naomi stands in the entry, just staring at me. Her stare is anything but friendly.

"Bath time," Valerie announces and points to the stairwell. None of the children argues, as a matter of fact, they all move up the stairs as if their lives depend on it. Valerie trades a glance with CJ and follows the children upstairs.

"Naomi," I say, and give her the slightest of nods. My hands are full of dirty dishes and my heart pounds in my throat. Sam moves to my side and a low growl emanates from her, but at least her teeth aren't bared. I can't say the same for the woman across the room.

"I heard you were back," she says. Her intentions are as clear in her mind as on her face.

"Don't," both CJ and I say at the same time, but it's too late.

Naomi launches, changing from human to tiger in mid-air and there's murder in her heart.

I don't defend myself, instead I brace for impact when Sam launches, catching Naomi mid-flight and knocking her off course. She misses me and slides into the wall with Sam's mouth wrapped around her front leg.

"Sam, back off!" I yell and transfer the dishes onto the counter, moving to intercept before Naomi turns her anger on my dog.

I catch her collar and yank.

"Drop it!" My command confuses both Sam and Naomi and she drops her grip. Blood speckles the white fur and Naomi hisses at me. Sam tries to lunge again, but I have a solid grasp on her. "No, Sam. Sit!"

CJ steps in front of me, blocking Naomi from another attack, while I try to calm Sam. When I glance back up, Naomi is back in human form, holding her bleeding arm.

Before I have a chance to speak, something connects with my back, knocking me flat on my stomach. I roll in time to see Sam getting ready to attack the other animal in the room.

"Stay," I yell, giving Sam the hand signal before I focus on the other cat on the attack. A white tiger with wings; a memory surfaces, shocking the name from my lips.

"Grace?" I say as I scramble backwards. Her paw swats towards me and I duck under it as the breeze ruffles through my hair.

"Stop this! Right now!"

Valerie's command halts everything, and we all turn our gaze toward the stairwell. Behind her stands Alex, his eyes wide and his jaw slack.

"Don't you dare step into my home with violent intent," she says, maneuvering herself between Grace and me.

"Do you know what he's done now?" Naomi asks with a hitching breath.

"I don't give a shit what you think he's done. He's family."

"So am I," Naomi growls back.

Valerie gives her a hard glare. "It's not the same."

Naomi's jaw clenched and her gaze moved to Grace pacing in front of me, her teeth on display in a feral snarl. She does one more pass in front of me before she transitions back to human form. I stare at her angry teenage features, so different from the five-year-old I left behind. All the forgiveness she had given back then is gone, replaced with a hostility that borders on hatred.

"He fucking closed Paradise Cove," Grace yelled. "Now I can never see my dad again!"

Valerie moves her gaze to mine. There is a measure of shock there, but she recovers after a moment.

"First of all, you watch your language under my roof... understand, young lady?"

Some of the fire in Grace calms, and her gaze moves to the stairwell where Alex stares at her, and then her eyes drop to the floor. Her cheeks burn red, and she gives Valerie a meek nod.

While Grace is humbled by Valerie's scolding, I climb to my feet and snap my fingers for Sam. She darts to me, positions herself just in front of my leg where she plants herself on her haunches, studying the dynamics in the room as acutely as I am.

"Did you bother to find out what happened, or are you assuming Tom just did it out of spite?"

"Val?" CJ says, calling her attention before she can get truly get wound up. "Naomi needs a little help." He points to the torn skin and the blood dripping and they trade places. It's a strategic move because the doorway behind Grace is now filled with three others. Michael and Damian's sons stand just outside the open sliders, and they all carry the same fury in their eyes as Grace.

I do not want to hurt anyone, but I'm starting to quake in that familiar way I do when I'm close to losing it. CJ glances over his shoulder at me and sends one word. *Breathe.*

I huff and give him the slightest of headshakes. He hasn't seen me in action. He doesn't know what happens when this shit inside me ignites. It's devastating, and it has a tendency to spin out of control.

Valerie gives me a quick glance as well before she delivers her healing mojo to Naomi. Naomi's audible flinch nearly echoes in the room's silence, and the broken skin mends.

"You can't keep fanning this hatred," Valerie says to Naomi. "It's poison, and it's deliberate. It's exactly what Lucifer wanted when he orchestrated Damian's death. Don't you get that? This is what he wants, for all of us to be divided."

God bless my sister-in-law. She might not be a genius, but she knows more about Lucifer's subterfuge than anyone in this room does. She knows his game plan even better than CJ, and my brother shared his body with the devil for months.

"He gave Tom no choice. Even if Damian had known what he was walking into, you really think he'd sacrifice Hannah for his own skin?"

Naomi lowers her eye to the floor, and she shakes her head.

"You would have done the same for any of your children," Valerie's voice softens. "Whether or not you admit it, you know in your heart what I'm saying is true."

Naomi looks over Valerie's shoulder at me, and I don't shy away from her gaze. I need her to see how much I regret my actions. I need her to understand that the moment Lucifer had Hannah, I was at his mercy.

"And I'm sure there is a damned good reason why Tom closed Paradise Cove."

"Actually," I interrupt Valerie because I don't want her to defend my actions. Not when that debacle resulted from my lack of control. "It was more of a reaction than any conscious decision." Heat fills my face and I unbutton my shirt, showing the fingernail welts on my skin over my heart. "Michael…" I start and shrug, jutting my chin towards where he stands. Every adult in the room understands what the welts mean. "At least I knocked you clear of the destruction."

Alex stood still on the steps, taking all this in, and finally others in the room besides Grace and I take notice.

"You should be upstairs," Valerie says.

He just stands, planted in place and when his eyes meet mine, he says, "You killed Grace's father?"

I nod.

"So, you're a murderer and a thief?"

I trade a glance with my brother before I look back at my nephew and nod.

"I don't want you to stay here."

"Okay," I answer, and I fully understand his aversion to having me under the same roof.

"You don't get to make that decision," CJ says, pointing at Alex. "Go upstairs and check on your sisters."

Alex spins and stomps up the stairs, leaving us in the tension layering the family room. Valerie has moved into a strategic position as well, blocking

Naomi from Sam and me the way CJ is blocking Grace.

"You don't need to protect me," I finally say when I realize what they are doing. "I'm perfectly capable of destroying everything on my own."

Everyone turns towards me.

"I am a living, breathing fuck up, so just stop protecting me, okay?"

I didn't realize how much anger and hostility is brewing under the surface, or the depth of my self-loathing, until this moment when it all bubbles to the surface.

"I'm not a victim," I add, glancing between Valerie and CJ. "I made the decision. The choice to damn my soul was mine, and mine alone. God help me, if I could turn back the clock, I would do the same goddamned thing, and you know what?"

Heads slowly shake.

"Hannah would still be dead."

I point at Michael. "You want your grace?" My question is framed in a growl.

"Tom," CJ has his palms facing me and his cautious tone sets my irritation switch on high.

"Let him try to take it," I snarl, as the fury swirls inside, and the dishes on the counter rattle.

It isn't until everyone takes a step back that I realize my control is shot. Sam whines, nudging my hand. I can't stay. I spin on my heel and slip by Naomi, heading for the front door with Sam at my side.

I get halfway down the front walkway, when I run into an invisible wall. My breath turns white on the cold air and I stare in front of me, counting my breaths, trying to calm the rabid beast that has taken over my soul.

"CJ, let me go," I say, once I've gotten control.

"You really want someone to kick your ass?" he asks.

I glance over my shoulder at him. "Why? You really think you have it in you?"

He closes the distance, and I turn meeting his glare.

"I never treated you like a victim," he snaps.

I let out a laugh. "You're kidding me, right? That's all you've ever done. We've never been on equal ground, CJ. You're always the fucking white knight and I'm the poor pitiful kid who needs to be taken care of, to be watched over. I've always been the victim in your eyes."

"That's bullshit and you know it," he says, and the spark of anger in his eyes matches mine.

"The only time you didn't treat me like a child was the day you transferred this curse to me, and it wasn't because you thought I could handle it. It was just so you wouldn't be alone in this. Well, great job, big brother. You put me in Lucifer's path. This shit show is yours to bear."

"You were already on Lucifer's hit list, Tom. I just made sure you had a fighting chance."

My fist swings intending to smash that smart ass look right off his fucking face. CJ blocks my swing and launches an attack of his own. All those years of being sparring partners come back to bite me in the ass. CJ knows my thought process as well as I know his, and this battle leaves both of us frustrated and unable to get a solid shot in.

The catalog of moves shuffles through my brain, and when he charges out of pure aggravation, I pull my next move from a more unorthodox defense list. I grab his shirt and plant my right foot on his hip, dropping onto my back and launching him over my head. I roll and climb to my feet before CJ catches his breath.

I step to his side, looking down at him, my breath huffs with exertion and he just lies there, staring at the stars, puffing just as hard as I am. After a full minute, he meets my gaze.

"I'm not a little kid anymore."

CJ utters a laugh. "No shit," he says and glances at the house. "We have an audience."

This is not the first time I've bested my brother. "Yeah, well, at least I finally have witnesses this time," I say and offer him my hand.

He stares at it and then up at me. "I never meant to treat you like a victim."

"I know you never meant to, but you did, whether you realized it or not." I sigh and pocket my hands since he isn't taking the offer of help.

"I'm sorry," he says and I nod, accepting his apology.

I kick at the dirt while CJ climbs to his feet.

"Lucifer orchestrated my downfall, and I walked right into it. I've had ten years to think about that night. Ten long years to figure out where I went so wrong. I had a choice, and it isn't what you think it is." I finally meet his gaze. "It wasn't the simple choice of Damian or Hannah. It was the choice of good versus evil." I keep his stare. "I chose the wrong path and there is no way back."

I shift my weight from foot to foot, looking everywhere but at him. "It's taken me a long time to come to terms with that, along with the fact I would do it again if I was presented with the same circumstances."

"It doesn't look like you've come to terms with any of this," CJ says and his eyebrows arch. "Seems to me you're still fighting."

I laugh. "Well, I've gotten to the point that I can look at myself in the mirror. Not saying I like what I see, mind you, but at least I can now look myself in the eye.”

We trade a smile, and I shrug, making a calculated decision.

“Sooner or later, I’m going to be the devil’s bitch. I’d rather like that to be as far off as I can possibly make it. In the meantime...” I grab him by the back of the neck while I use my other hand to extract both Michael’s and Gabriel’s grace from my core. CJ struggles, but by my sheer will alone, I hold him still.

The combined grace is blinding, and with both my hand and my mind, I shove it inside my brother. The transfer takes seconds, but the effect on CJ stuns me. Every cell emits light, and his eyes roll back as it engulfs him. My mental hold is the only thing keeping him upright at this moment, and I hang on while fear tears through my insides.

The lightning display surrounding us creates a tinny taste in my mouth and I’m not sure if it’s just the electricity in the air, or the combination of the current along with my building fear. Flashes illuminate wings, but not the white ones I’ve seen him sport in the past. No, these are golden with a shine so bright I have to look away.

I have a second to wonder if the neighbors are witnessing this spectacle, and then CJ’s eyes snap back in place, meeting my gaze.

“What the hell did you do that for?” he breathes, as the light encompassing him fades.

“A true trinity, with trinity grace, makes you unstoppable. Now you have everything you need to win.” I step away, letting go mentally and physically. “Especially, if I fall.”

He keeps my gaze. We both know what happens if Lucifer gets hold of me, but at least now it’s only his grace that’s subject to being ripped out of me, and not a trinity of grace like it had been a few moments ago.

"You want to let go of that mental hold you have on my dog?"

CJ's lips twitch into a hint of a smile and he gives a nod. Sam streaks across the distance, winding around my legs in a frantic display, and just like that, the tension between my brother and me is gone.

I can't say the same for the rest of the crew.

Chapter 6

"WHY ARE YOU LETTING him stay here?" Alex's voice echoes through the house, and I close my eyes, rolling towards the wall and covering my head with the extra pillow.

After our little spectacle outside, I'd begged off and headed to the guest room. I'd stood in the doorway and my chest squeezed. The last time I'd slept in this location was with Raven, after her father had been caught, and the memories just magnified the nothingness gripping me.

Arguments rage until doors slam, and I lift the pillow only to find Sam's wet nose in my face.

"You need to go out now?"

She licks my face and I sigh, pulling on a pair of sweats and my zip up sweatshirt. Quietly, I climb down the stairs and open the slider to the backyard. Instead of waiting inside, I cross onto the cold patio stones in my bare feet. The chill grips my heels and I move onto the grass, but that's no better. I move towards the rock wall and take a seat, leaning against one of the posts while Sam inspects the lawn.

The sliver of a moon sends light dancing off the waves and the calm cadence of the sea keeps me in place, despite the nip in the air. After a few minutes, I know I'm not alone and I turn my head, staring into Grace's bloodshot eyes a few feet away. I'm surprised Sam didn't approach her, but then again, she doesn't have murderous intent in her posture or her mind.

I wave towards the rock wall, silently inviting her to sit with me.

"I'm sorry," she whispers.

"Don't be. You have every right to hate me."

She let a small laugh out.

"That's the thing; I can't seem to dredge up the will to hate you."

I turn my gaze back out to the sea. "That makes one of us." I let the soothing sound of the waves come between us. Finally, I sigh and look at her. "What changed from earlier this evening?"

It was her turn to look out at the ocean. "I remembered."

"You remembered what?"

"I remembered the promise I made to Hannah."

My throat tightens and I'm almost afraid to ask, but I force myself to. "What promise was that?"

"She said I needed to promise not to be mad, because what you did, you did to save me."

I chuckle under my breath at my daughter's innocence. "Grace, I did what I did to get my daughter out alive. I knew it was wrong, and I didn't care."

"If you didn't care, why didn't you give Lucifer what he wanted?"

I chewed on the inside of my lip. Sam trotted up to us and sniffed Grace cautiously, giving me a minute to figure out how to frame the answer.

"Grace, I wasn't thinking of you or your family. I wasn't even thinking of Hannah. I was thinking of myself and no one else," I say in barely a whisper. "I'm not the flawed saint my daughter made me out to be. I'm the demon in the closet."

She blinks a few times, and her expression darkens.

"If I wasn't so goddamned self-centered, I would never have risked your father's life or brought him within a hundred miles of Lucifer, despite the consequences." I offer a shrug and cross my arms. "The truth isn't pretty, sweetheart."

Her gaze narrows and her lips thin.

"When did you start to turn tiger?" I ask, trying to distract her building anger.

Her lips rub together for a moment and then she answers me.

"When I started my period." Her words are clipped and short.

"That must have been a joy."

My response pulls a bark of a laugh from her. "It sucked, and until today, I had successfully hidden my affliction from Alex."

I let out a heavy sigh. "It's not an affliction. It might just save your life someday."

"I'm a fucking freak."

"We're all freaks, if you hadn't noticed." I wave towards the house.

"What do you care? I thought you said you were the bad guy?"

I keep quiet and just level a stare that communicates 'really?' She shifts in her seat and flips her hair over her shoulder, slamming home a memory of what she was like at five. I can't help the smile that finds its way to my lips.

"You are about as evil as your damned dog," she says, her words loaded with teen-age attitude.

"Sam's a pussycat." I reach out and give my dog a pat.

She stares at me for a second and then laughs. This time it starts soft but soon it's the snorting kind of laughter that's echoing off the surrounding rocks.

"Shhh. You want to wake everyone?" I scold but I smile.

"You aren't the badass you pretend to be," she finally says and gets to her feet. "And at least you own your mistakes. That's rare, you know."

"So, it seems."

She takes a couple of steps and pauses. "I still miss Hannah," she adds without turning.

"So do I."

I watch her go and embrace the familiar ache in the center of my chest. I close my eyes and memories of Hannah and Grace running around this back yard roll through my mind. Their laughter still rings in my ears, and I clench my jaw against the burn at the back of my throat.

Sam nudges me.

"You about ready to go inside and catch some sleep?" The slow sweep of her tail answers and I climb to my feet, moving across the backyard at a fast pace on feet numbed by the cold.

Chapter 7

SAM WAKES ME AT some ungodly hour and I brush my teeth before I head out for a morning walk with her. Long Sands beach at low tide is such a relaxing walk, especially with the sun coming up over the ocean. It's reviving, and even the cool wind whipping off the water invigorates me. I forgot the sense of peace the Atlantic Ocean brings me. It's been way too long, and I can't imagine settling down anywhere else.

It's early enough on the beach to let Sam walk without her leash and I unclasp the hook. She glances up at me as if she's unsure about leaving my side and investigating the unfamiliar surroundings.

"It's okay, girl. You can check things out."

Her tail wags and I continue walking. Sam runs ahead of me with her nose to the sand before she stops, looking over her shoulder to make sure I'm still in the area. Her concern makes me smile, but I continue my leisurely gait. She stays within twenty feet of me at all times and when other dogs approach, she does a cursory sniff and then she's on her way.

"Tom?"

My gaze snaps up from Sam. A familiar face is walking towards me, but I'm at a loss for a name. I smile anyway.

"Hi," I say.

"Austin's going to shit," she says and the name snaps in place as she stops in front of me.

"How are you, Paige?" I ask.

"Pretty good. When did you get back?"

"Two nights ago."

A large and very wet Alaskan Malamute, with one blue eye and one brown eye, trots up to Paige and drops a ball at her feet. Sam slides between us, positioning herself in front of me in that protective stance I'm used to.

I reach down, stroke her head, and she looks up at me.

"It's okay, girl," I say and glance up at Paige. She has the ball in her hand and pitches it into the water. The massive dog bounds after it and Sam just watches.

"Nice dog," I say and Paige glances at Sam.

"She's beautiful," she says and crouches down offering her hand.

"Sam, this is Paige," I introduce, and she sniffs Paige's hand.

"Wow, she's really trained well," she says, looking up at me as she pets Sam.

"I guess."

"I can't get Goliath to stay by my side like she does," she says and smiles, standing while her dog comes bounding back.

"Goliath, very appropriate name." I smile and her dog finally takes notice of Sam and the sniffing begins until Sam issues a low warning growl. "How old is he?"

"Five. And we really thought he'd calm down by now, but he really hasn't." She laughs and tosses the ball again. "He has pulled me down a couple of times, but he's been good lately."

"Sam's been with me from a puppy and she's kind of kept me alive," I say as Sam nudges my hand and I stroke her head, scratching behind her ear.

"So, I imagine you were successful?" She looks out over the ocean before bringing her gaze back to mine.

"All the portals are closed, if that's what you're asking," I say and she nods slowly. "However, there was a loophole none of us were aware of."

Her pleasant smile fades. "What loophole?"

"Our, um, enemy is locked topside, so we are all still in danger."

Her face pales. "How the hell did that happen?"

I shift and shrug. "They forgot to mention that he had to be present when the last portal was closed. He wasn't, and I shut it down without knowing."

A pained sigh escapes her. "You know we barely got away with our lives, right?"

"Yes. CJ told me what happened when he contacted me about the house." I slide my hands in my pocket. "I understand Austin's a doctor now?" I deftly change the subject.

The genuine smile forms again. "Yes, and he works here in York now."

"That's what Val was saying yesterday. What about you? What are you doing?"

"I work in the Ogunquit Museum."

"Nice." I can't think of anything else to say and I shift my weight.

"We got married a few years ago." She raises her hand showing off the gleaming diamond.

"So, he finally popped the question. I wondered if he'd ever get the nerve up."

She raises her eyebrows with a laugh. "It took him entirely too long, but yes. He finally grew a pair."

I laugh and a gust chills me to the point I shove my hands in my pockets. She shivers as well.

"Well..." I start.

"You want to see the house?" she asks, pointing her thumb over her shoulder.

I never saw the finished product before I left and I shrug, even though I'm curious as hell.

"Come on, Austin will be happy to see that you're okay."

"All right," I say and she whistles for Goliath.

He trots to within a few feet and shakes the water out of his fur, spraying Paige, Sam, and me, before going to Paige. She snaps on the leash and starts up the beach. I keep pace, with Sam between us.

"Damn, that is a really special dog," she says as we reach the stairs.

"That she is," I agree and wave her forward. We follow on the narrow sidewalk until the sidewalk disappears on Nubble Road. I stay behind Paige with Sam on my right side. She never strays and I have to smile as Goliath seems to be distracted by everything he sees.

We stop in front of the property where I spent my life with Raven, before she died. The house looks completely different from the quaint cape that sat there before, and I smile at the realization of the design I worked on with the builders. The multiple roof lines of the California Bungalow style is much more pleasing than the plain lines the house used to have.

"It looks fantastic," I say.

"It's a little weathered," she says, "but outside of replacing some shingles, it's been a great place to live."

Something in her words makes me take a closer look at her. "Paige, I don't want the house back," I say, just to settle her nerves and her creased brow smooths. "I knew I was giving it up when I signed the papers."

She looks at the ground and then up at me with a small smile. "We love it here," she says and heads into the garage. "You can bring your dog inside if you want," she adds when I pause at the entry.

She towels off her malamute. The moment Paige opens the door, the dog darts inside. Sam looks up at me and I swear her eyebrows rise at the behavior of the other dog. I press my lips against a smirk and follow Paige inside.

"Austin," Paige yells. "I found an old friend of yours on the beach!"

Austin steps out from the front of the house and his aura is as bright as the rest of the angel kin. I smile and give him a head nod.

"Holy shit! How the hell are you?" he asks, crossing to me, offering his hand and I shake it.

"I'm well, thank you." I give a glance around as we step farther into the home. The kitchen is wide open to the family room, as I had arranged. I never liked the separation between rooms, and this set up was as light and inviting as I had hoped. The back wall is almost entirely made of glass and the view is just as spectacular as I remembered.

"I'm going to clean up for work," Paige says and disappears upstairs.

"That's right, you never saw the finished product," Austin says.

"No. I never did, but I have to admit, it came out much better than I ever imagined."

"Then let me give you a tour," he says, waving me farther into the house. We walk from room to room and my mind goes from pleased to remembering every little thing I did for Hannah. The familiar sadness hits when I stand outside what was to be her room. A lump forms as I scan the mural of the Disney Castle.

"We never changed the decorations in here because someday, we'll have kids," he says.

Sam nudges my hand, picking up the melancholy that drifts over me. I scratch her ear and say, "Hopefully you have girls, because that would be a little much for a boy."

He laughs and nods, taking me back to the great room. "Can I get you something to drink?"

"Nah, I'm good."

"You sure? I just brewed a fresh pot of coffee?"

I glance at the pot of liquid energy and think about my walk back to CJ's. "Coffee might not be a bad idea," I say, and step up to the island while he fixes two cups of java.

"Cream and sugar?"

"Yes, both, please," I answer, glancing out at the backyard. Hannah and I had walked through the house a couple of times during the construction, but my last solid memory here was dumping Raven's ashes over the bluff.

"So, are you just visiting?" he asks as he passes the cup.

"No, I'm here to stay. I finished closing the portals."

He smiles and his eyes light up.

"It's not all good," I reply to his reaction. "Lucifer is stuck topside. They never mentioned he had to be there when I closed the last one." I shake my head in disgust. "So, we are pretty much in the same boat as before."

He closes his eyes and his chin dips to his chest. "I thought…"

"You thought you were free and clear the minute you saw me."

He nods and meets my gaze. "He's been powering up, too."

"So, I heard." I take a sip of the coffee.

"I held off having kids because I was betting on you closing the portals," he snaps.

"Sorry." I sigh.

"I'm not snapping at you. I'm just pissed at this whole thing. We barely made it out of Dartmouth, and I've been looking over my shoulder ever since."

"I don't have a clue how many of us are left, but I know when that source dries out, he's bringing the fight here."

"Have you talked to Naomi about who on that list is still alive?"

"No. She's tracking the list?"

He nods. "Apparently, Damian set up a program that posts an alert when someone dies. She knows the exact number of us who are left, along with where we are. You should talk to her."

"I'm not sure she's going to want to talk to me," I say.

"Why would you say that?"

I open my mouth and close it, studying him. "You don't know."

"Know what?"

I run my hand through my hair. "Shit. I would think after all this time, someone would have said more about why I took off."

"After your daughter died, CJ asked you to close the portals for him," he says with a crease between his eyes.

"No one told you what happened to Damian?"

Creases appear on his forehead and his eyebrows lower in confusion. "I know he died."

"I killed Damian."

His eyes widen and he steps back.

"Lucifer wanted his grace back in exchange for my daughter's life."

Bewilderment returns and his mind circles on how that had anything to do with me killing Damian.

"Damian harbored Lucifer's grace as well as Michael's and Gabriel's. I had to steal it for Lucifer."

Still, he did not get what that means.

"I had to rip out Damian's heart and give it to Lucifer," I finally spell it out. "Not my finest moment, but once I had it in my hand, I realized if I gave it to that bastard, we would all die. So, I ate his heart instead of handing it over."

"You're shitting me," Austin says with a laugh.

"No. That's how you steal grace."

His smile fades and the color in his face pales. "You ate his heart?"

I nod. "Hannah died anyway. And CJ didn't ask me to go. I went because it was my only chance to redeem myself, but considering I fucked up by leaving Lucifer on earth, I'm still damned."

Austin slides back until he's leaning on the counter next to the kitchen sink, putting as much distance between us as he can. His clinician's mind runs down all the psychosis' he might be dealing with and I chuckle, sipping my coffee.

"I'm not crazy. I was desperate, and a desperate man will do anything to keep his child safe."

"But in your case it backfired," he says still keeping his distance.

"Yes." I stare into my coffee and again, Sam nudges my hand and I glance down at her. "I'm okay," I say and rub her head before I meet Austin's gaze. "I should go, but thank you for the information. I did not know he set up a watch system."

I turn to leave the way I came in and stop. "If we know he's coming, I'll make sure someone calls you. It might be safer for everyone to be in one place."

"Why, so he can slaughter us all in one shot?"

I glance over my shoulder at him. "No. So he doesn't slaughter you before he comes to get his grace back."

Austin gulps and I give him a sarcastic smile.

"I'll catch you later." I take my leave before I say anything else. Sam trots next to me and I move faster on the way back. Sam's a good sport and keeps up, but by the time we walk in the door at CJ's, I can tell the old girl is tired. I give her food and water, wait until she is finished doing her business outside, and settled into a light sleep before I hear movement upstairs indicating the house is just waking up.

I slip outside and cross to Naomi's, and I stand at the back door for a moment, wondering how prudent this is. Last night she wanted nothing more than to rip me to shreds. I lift my hand and knock, hoping I'm not opening myself up for catastrophe.

She opens the door and the pleasant look on her face sours. "What do you want?"

"Austin said you had a program that's tracking how many angel decedents are still alive?"

She blinks and crosses her arms before she gives me a nod.

"And neither you nor CJ told them what I did?"

She presses her lips together and looks out over the ocean, shaking her head. "We didn't think it was his business."

I let that digest a moment. "Do you know how many descendants are left?"

She nods and waves me inside. Michael is sitting in front of the computer and the tightness of his neck and shoulders screams aggravation.

"Let Tom see," Naomi says, and Michael glances over his shoulder at me before he slides the chair away, inviting me to take a closer look.

Red dots fill the map of the world. There are a few green clusters in Central America, a few in Mexico, and then a concentrated cluster in York. The number tally at the bottom reads forty-five, and the screen refreshes. Another dot turns red, and the number decreases to forty-four.

"Jesus," I whisper.

Michael glances up at me. "Even he wouldn't be able to help us now."

My gaze snaps to his and he runs his hands through his hair.

"With the rate he's going through the list, he isn't alone. He's got his guard with him, which means we have a slim chance of winning, even with giving your brother a trinity of grace."

"We have no issues toasting demons," I say and straighten.

"They aren't like any demon you've ever encountered. They are his elite guard. The oldest and strongest demons, and if they are feasting on angel blood along with Lucifer, I'm afraid your powers might not be enough."

"How long?" I nod towards the screen, and Michael gives me a shrug.

"A week. Two weeks at the most." He looks up at me. "I honestly don't know. I have no idea how fast he's been moving, so my guess is only as good as Naomi's information."

"It would take about four days of straight driving to get from Costa Rica to Maine without stopping. So, unless he wants to give up the rest of that angel blood, it's at least four days."

"He has access to a private plane," I say.

Naomi's gaze jumps to the screen and the fact that the dots are clustered doesn't settle well with either of us. He has four plane hops to decimate the bloodline before he heads to York.

"I don't know, then," she says, less certain this time.

"Well, keep an eye out and let me know when the last one goes red. That's when we will need to warn everyone."

They nod and I head back to the house. CJ's tooling around the kitchen and I take a seat at the breakfast bar.

"Why did you tell Austin you asked me to go close the portals?"

CJ stops and faces me. "Would you rather I told the truth?"

"Actually, I would. It's the same as treating me like a victim. You're making excuses for my actions. Don't."

"I'm sorry; I was just trying to avoid the conversation." He turns back to the stove and flips the egg, letting it sizzle on the other side before sliding it off onto a plate. He turns off the burner and takes a seat.

I get his aversion. No one wants to admit their brother murdered someone. It just isn't socially acceptable. "Did you know about Damian's tracking machine?" I ask, hooking my thumb towards Naomi's house.

He nods with his mouth full and takes a sip of juice. "Yeah. I was going to suggest we look at that today to see where Lucifer is right now."

"Central America. I've been over there. There are less than fifty of us now."

His eyes widen. "He's already swept South America?"

"Yes."

"Oh, man," he whispers, and stares at his food. CJ slowly pushes the plate of half-eaten eggs away. "I'm not ready for this."

"No one ever is." I give him a tight smile and file the facts about Lucifer's guards for a conversation we need to have later.

"We have a couple of days. Let me have today to get my head clear, okay?" he asks.

"Sure, what do you need from me?"

He stares at the countertop and then looks up. "We are going to need some serious groceries if we are going to be holed up in the house for the next few days."

I smile. "I can run to the store after I clean up, as long as you have a car I can borrow. I also need to run to Kittery to get some clothes."

"Sure," he says. "I'll put together a list, and you're going to need to stop at the hardware store, too, just in case."

I cock my head at him.

"You'll understand when you see the list."

"No problem. And it's okay if I leave Sam here?" Sam's head lifts at the mention of her name.

"That is no problem at all. She's a good dog."

Sam yawns and puts her head back down and I head upstairs to shower and shave.

The warm water pounds the back of my shoulders, and I take my time washing up. My nephew is still pissed that I'm staying in the house, and I can't think of what to do to turn that around. Maybe something at the store will present itself, but I'm not sure what a ten-year-old is into these days.

I climb down the stairs, and everyone is up and sitting at the breakfast bar helping CJ with the list.

"I can also pick up some movies if you'd like." I say and get a nasty look in return from Alex.

"We've got streaming movies, so that's unnecessary," Valerie says, and glances at her watch. "I need to go. Be good for your father today." She looks straight at Alex when she says it and he drops his eyes to the paper in front of him. "Love you, hon," she adds, and catches a kiss from CJ before she waves her fingers at me and disappears out the garage door.

"Here's the list, and the keys to my truck," CJ says, swiveling on the seat and holding out both items.

A quick scan of the list tells me the kids might have gotten to CJ before Valerie did, and the list of junk food covers half the page. I glance over the edge at CJ and he shrugs. Reading down the list, I get to the rock salt, which explains the hardware store. I give him a nod and start for the door. Sam gets to her feet and I turn back.

"You're staying here," I point at her. "You've earned a day of rest."

Her ears drop and she looks totally dejected, almost to the point I give in, but with the number of stores I need to hit, it wouldn't be fair to leave her in the car.

"She'll be fine," CJ says. "We'll keep her busy." He smiles and I nod, taking my leave.

AFTER LIVING OUT OF a duffel bag for years, I'm hard pressed to buy more than what can carry me over for a few days. I chuckle as I glance at my meager pile of clothes. Just a couple of pairs of jeans and a half dozen shirts are balanced on my arm, but with the shit still hanging over my head, I don't want to stock up for nothing.

The morbid thought sours my mood and I glance around the store as I wait for the next cashier to free up. Once I have my clothing and slide into the truck, I have one detour in mind, and I swing into the toy store outlet, not sure if a gift would help, but it couldn't hurt.

I debate on what to get and I travel back and forth between the boy section and the girl section so many times that finally one of the salesclerks comes to my rescue.

"Can I help you?"

"I have no idea what to get my ten-year-old nephew." I say. "And I didn't want to show up empty-handed for my seven-year-old nieces either."

He smiles and turns, leading me down a few aisles before he stops in the section with all things nerf.

He pulls down a couple of nerf guns. "You will want to get the refills because these things get lost easily. I suggest getting them for both the kids, they will have a blast."

"Really?"

"Yes. I have two girls and a boy and they constantly ambush each other."

I look at the one he hands me and then up at the others. "How about the Zombie strike one?"

"Good choice. Two?"

"Three, my brother has twins."

He brings me up to the register and checkout, and I request gift bags to go along with them. With all three packaged up, I put them in the cab of the truck with my new clothes, and then I'm on my way to the supermarket.

My cart screams party and I huff as I toss in yet another bag of chips and as I take the turn to hit the soda aisle, I bang carts with another shopper.

"Sorry," I say and look up.

"Thankfully you don't drive as sloppily as you push a shopping cart," Bridget says and I laugh. She eyes the contents and then looks at me. "Think you have enough junk?"

I turn the list in her direction. "CJ's, not mine."

An awkward tension builds between us, and she starts to navigate around me.

"Can we talk?"

She slowly shakes her head. "I can't Tom, not with what's at stake."

Her words belie the colors swirling in her aura and my jaw tightens. "You can't just write me off," I hiss under my breath.

"I have for ten years," she says and walks away with her cart as if I'm a complete stranger.

It burns, and I turn into the soda aisle, nearly pitching the boxes of soda onto the lower shelf of the cart. Eventually, she would have to listen to reason, but with the cold shoulder, today would not be that day.

I focus on the rest of the list, but just knowing she is in the store is distracting. With my cart nearly overflowing, I step into the checkout line. Bridget just happens to be in front of me and as I stack my groceries on the belt, she gives me a dirty look.

"What?" I say in response, opening my arms wide. "This is a public place, right?"

Her lips press together and the fire of anger burns in her eyes. I continue stacking, and when the cashier states her total, Bridget reaches into her back pocket, pulling out her credit card holder. She unzips it and pulls out the few cards enclosed, shuffling through them.

Flares of panic color her aura as she shuffles again and now looks in the empty pouch.

"I, um, it seems I've left my card at home," she says, as her cheeks bloom.

"I got this," I say, and pull out my card.

"No." Her glare is enough, but I hand the card to the cashier.

"Don't be difficult. This saves you a trip back," I say and the cashier ping-pongs her gaze to Bridget.

"I'd rather have to drive across the country and back than take your money," Bridget says, and the cashier's lips form a shocked 'o' before she looks at me.

"Charge the card," I say with authority, and she swipes it through the machine without any further argument.

"Damn it, Tom," Bridget says, and her hands clench into fists.

"You're welcome," I say, and she lets out a derisive huff, stomping away from the line.

The only word I catch is 'asshole,' and I glance at the cashier and her equally wide-eyed stare.

"She's a little mad at me," I whisper and finish stacking the conveyor belt.

The cashier chuckles. "I would say so." She hands me the card back and rings up my bill. By the time I get to the parking lot, Bridget is gone, and I shake my head at her angry display. I am so tempted to swing by the house and give her hell, but I have some frozen foods sitting in the truck bed that might end up as mush if I do that, so I head to the last stop.

The hardware store.

It seems rock salt is pretty scarce in late March and all I can get is the last five-pound bag, not a twenty-pound bag CJ asked for. When I pull into the garage, the first things I pull from the cab are the gifts, along with my clothing.

I cross to the coffee table where the kids are working hard and deposit the three bags right in the center. "You can open them once we have all the groceries inside," I say, before they can grab the gifts. All three pairs of eyes look up at me and then, collectively, they get up and head out to the garage to help with the groceries.

I trade a grin with CJ, and we step out, grabbing the lion's share of bags before coming back inside with the crew.

"You can't buy me," Alex mumbles, but the minute he opens the bag and pulls out the Nerf gun, I can see some softening in his hard features. "I get to shoot you with this, right?" he asks with narrow eyes.

"If you can hit me, sure." I say, and glance down at Sam as she stretches and trots over to me. "I didn't forget you," I say, and rummage through the grocery bags for the dog bones I bought.

The girls both grin at their guns and turn their gaze on Alex. "We can play zombie wars!" Amber or Arianna exclaims.

"Dad, can we stop for the day?" Alex asks, inspecting his new toy.

"Sure. Why don't you take those downstairs, though?"

He didn't need to say things twice. They grab their gift bags and bolt to the basement.

I'm thrilled they like the gifts, and I grab my clothing bag and bring it up to the guest room before I return to help CJ put the groceries away.

"What time does Val get back?" I ask as I unload the bags onto the countertop.

"Thursday's are her late day," he says. "So, she won't be home till almost eight tonight."

I glance at the clock and it's a little after two in the afternoon. "I ran into Bridget at the store. She's still pissed off at me."

"She'll get over it." CJ grabs the soda boxes and slides them into the pantry before he takes a seat on the couch, picking up the papers and a pen, correcting his kid's work.

I slide onto the couch across from him.

"I know you said you wanted today to get your head together, but there's one other thing you need to know."

He looks up from the paper, waiting for me to finish.

"I guess Lucifer is traveling with his guards. From what Michael said, they aren't like normal demons."

"And?"

"And they can't be turned to dust as easily as normal demons."

He slowly lowers the paper.

"Especially if they are drinking angel blood along with Lucifer."

"So, things might get bloodier than we expected." He leans back in the couch cushion and closes his eyes.

"Michael's worried. So, yes. I think we're looking at a serious beating."

"That's just great," he mutters, and picks up the papers again, focusing on the kid's schoolwork instead of the inevitable.

I let him have his space, but I know what I just told him is scalding his insides as much as it is mine. I stand and cross to the kitchen to find something to munch on. Nacho chips, cheese dip and a beer sounds like a good snack, so I grab two bottles and carry my bounty to the coffee table, setting one beer in front of my brother before opening the chip bag and dip.

He sends a sideways glance at the beer and then looks at me.

"What else are we going to do?" I ask when he raises an eyebrow. "Besides, it's not like it's ten in the morning."

"I can't go and get drunk. I've got three kids to watch tonight," he says.

"Relax. It's just one beer." I kick my feet back on the table and Sam jumps up next to me, laying her head on my lap.

Begrudgingly, CJ reaches out and snatches the beer, giving me the evil eye as he takes the first sip. "You could have gotten a bowl," he nods towards the chip bag in my lap.

I offer him the open end of the bag and he grabs a handful. The cheese dip ends up on the corner of the coffee table between us.

"How's the studio working out?" I nod to the closed door to the right of the television, trying to take the edge off the swirl building in his mind.

He sighs. "Good," he says. "It gives me that needed outlet, since I haven't toured in a long time."

"I saw you on an international charity telethon about a year ago," I say. I remember that one because Sam and I had just gotten back from closing a portal and had some bruises from the beasts we encountered. We had just chilled in the hotel room with ice packs and whatever I could find of interest on television. Surprised to catch the airing in the middle of China was an understatement, but it had been one of those moments that made me glad I was the one risking my ass as opposed to my brother. The world needed him more than it needed me.

Before he can comment on the wandering narrative in my head, the air shifts and the whistle of a nerf bullet whizzes by my face and hits CJ's beer dead center as he draws a sip. I turn and the arsenal of nerf comes at a clip fast enough, so my diving roll away from the couch is speckled with foam.

I stand, assessing the damage... at least a dozen of the sticky nerf arrows are now tacked on my shirt. Alex, Amber, and Arianna stand from their hiding spot behind the couch with grins so wide I have to laugh.

"We got you!" Amber exclaims.

"That's because you ambushed me," I say, pulling the darts off and offering them to the kids. Even Sam has a few sticking to her fur. I have a moment, wishing what was coming for us was as benign as these nerf darts, but I know better than to waste a wish on a lost cause.

So, for now, I decide to embrace the lighthearted mischief blooming in the children's eyes.

"You don't happen to have any of these things hanging around that we could use," I ask CJ, and he shakes his head.

"Well, then, it's time to rectify that." I put my hand out. "Can I borrow your keys again?"

CJ tosses me the keys and Sam gets to her feet. I glance at the kids.

"Alex, you feel like coming to the store with me?" I ask and he glances at his father before looking back at me. He's torn, he still doesn't trust me. "Neither of us bite," I add as Sam stands by my side wagging her tail.

After a moment of complete indecision, he nods and puts his nerf gun on the counter before following me to the truck. I open the back door for Sam, and Alex climbs into the passenger seat.

Quiet encompasses the cab, and I glance at Alex.

"I'm sorry if I disrupted your life," I start, and he just looks out the window. "I missed out on watching you and your sisters grow up."

"Why did you even come home?" he mutters under his breath.

"Because I thought it was done and everyone was safe. Guess I blew that one."

Alex narrows his eyes at me. "My dad doesn't even have a picture of you at the house."

"That's because our homes were blown up before I left town." I say. "The only pictures I have of the family are in Wolfboro."

"Wolfeboro?"

I nod. "I still have a house there. At least I think I do," I clarify. I really don't know if that house is still standing, but I would imagine my real estate agent would have told me otherwise, and I have consistently paid the upkeep bills over the years. "Your dad never took you guys over to the lake?"

Alex shakes his head.

"Well, this summer, we will have to take a trip. If I recall correctly, I have videos of when your dad and I were kids."

"Really?" His eyes spark with interest. "I'd like to see what he was like at my age."

"Your dad was always the good kid," I say and send a wink in his direction. "I was the one that dragged him into trouble."

"So, you've always been a troublemaker?" he asks.

"Kind of. But I had some bad stuff happen when I was a little younger than you are, and it screwed me up."

"Like what?" There isn't a hint of sarcasm in his question. It was asked with all the innocence of a child, and I sigh.

"I was kidnapped by a serial killer." I glance over at him. "Obviously, I survived, but that's only because of the magic your mom now holds."

He is quiet but I can hear the questions plaguing him.

"Go ahead, ask your questions," I say and glance at him. "But you might not want the answers."

"What did he do to you?"

"He practiced surgery on his victims without knocking them out."

Alex's eyes widen and his jaw loosens as he stares at me. "What kind of surgery?" His voice is small as he whispers the question.

"He cut out my spleen, and he butchered my tongue." I say. "I had to learn sign language and used my hands to talk for twenty years until my wife died and willed her tongue to me."

His horrified glance locks on me, but I don't look his way.

"I knew real monsters existed long before we ever knew Lucifer was real."

"Why didn't my dad stop him?" he finally asks.

I glance at Alex as I pull into a parking spot. "If your father had known where to find me, none of it would have happened. I didn't have this back then." I tap my temple. "And I didn't know how to get a message to him." I turn the vehicle off and stare ahead for a moment. "Are you okay?" I ask, glancing his way.

Alex nods. "I didn't know." He gives me a forced smile.

"It's okay." I mess up his hair. "Now let's go buy out the entire stock of zombie nerf guns and whatever else you think would be fun."

True to my word, we buy the remaining guns and as many refills as they have, and we head home to take this zombie war game to the next level.

By the time Valerie rolls in, the house is littered with nerf darts, some still sticking to each of us, and we are all lounging on the couch with the remnants of homemade pizza on the counter and discarded plates on the coffee table. In short, the place is a disaster, and a twinge of guilt bites me.

I rise and gather the plates, offering her a tired smile.

"Sorry about the mess," I mumble, as she takes her coat off and crosses to grab the last few pieces of pizza that we saved for her.

"I'm not upset. I know you and CJ will clean it up," she says, smiling around the pizza. "Did you guys have a fun day today?" she asks, focusing on her kids.

"Yeah," Alex says. "Uncle Tom got us all nerf guns and we played zombie war most of the day."

She glances my way with a nod of approval and I smile. My nephew still has some reservations about me, but today did a great deal to thaw some of the frosty attitude.

Overall, it was a good day, and right now, I'll settle for as many of these as I can rack up before hell comes knocking on our door.

Chapter 8

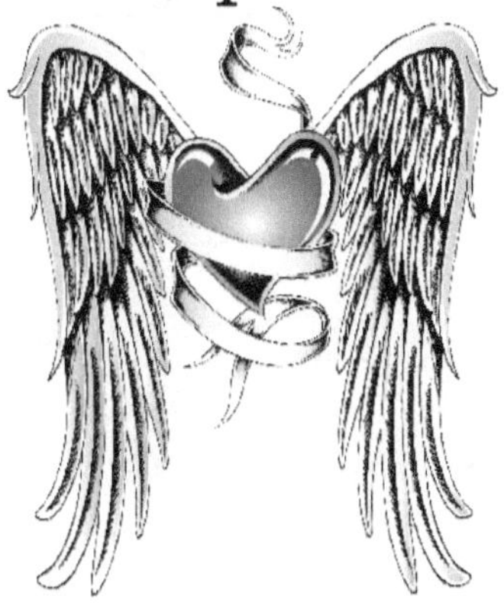

THE NEXT MORNING, I wake before anyone else and tinker in the kitchen, making a pot of coffee. The light knock on the door interrupts my morning stupor and I look around as if I expect someone else to answer it.

No one else is awake.

The second round of knocks comes, and I slide off the bar stool and cross to the door, pausing a moment to do a security scan with my mind. What I find on the other side makes me yank the door open.

Bridget meets my bewildered gaze.

"I, um, I just came by to say thank you for helping me out at the grocery store yesterday. I'm sorry I was such a bitch," she says and shifts her feet. When she tries to hand me the cash to cover the bill, I shake my head.

"Look, you don't have to pay me back and you certainly don't have to apologize to me," I say and open the door wide for her. "If you want to pay me back, why don't you just come in and have a cup of coffee with me and we can call it even."

Her eyes dart from the kitchen entry and back to me.

"No one's up yet," I answer her unspoken question. "It's just me and Sam puttering around the kitchen. How about that cup of coffee?" I wave toward the back of the house and after a moment of hesitation, she crosses the threshold.

"I just didn't expect you..." Her hands flutter towards my open shirt as she speaks and she can't seem to find the words to finish her sentence. Her entire demeanor amuses me.

"Why are you nervous?"

A high-pitched laugh escapes and I close the door behind her, placing my hand on the small of her back to guide her into the kitchen. Just the touch spreads warmth through me and she glances down at the contact, and then her gaze lands on my lips for a brief second before finding my eyes. Her aura is a chaotic mess, including flares of iridescent pink, and she just shakes her head at me.

I drop my hand and a chill builds between us.

"I shouldn't have sprung April on you like that," she says and takes a seat at the breakfast bar.

"I probably should have called first," I admit and grab a mug for her coffee. I fix it from memory and slide it across the marble to her. I figure if I keep the stone between us, I won't be tempted to screw this up by making a move that really isn't welcome.

"You should have called a long time ago."

"I walked right into that, didn't I?"

She doesn't answer. Instead, she just takes a sip of her coffee and her gaze travels down to my bare chest. I can almost feel her caress as her eyes move lower to the waistline of my low riding sweats. Suddenly, she looks away and takes a deep breath.

Now, all I can think about is that last night before I left. I'm trying like hell to concentrate on this moment, but my brain keeps going back ten years to how she tasted under my lips.

"Damn it," I mutter and shake my head, trying to drive the thoughts away, but it's difficult since that memory ran through my head at least a dozen times a day since I left. By now, it was over-glorified, embellished with enough fantasy to confuse what was real and what was my brain making up shit just to grasp onto her, and each revisiting of that night drilled feelings for Bridget farther into me, deeper than I ever anticipated.

"What?" she asks, leaning away from the counter, her eyes now guarded.

"I really want to get this countertop dirty."

Her mouth pops open and her cheeks flare pink.

Heat fills my face as well, because when I went to answer her, those were *not* the words forming in my head.

"I'm sorry. That was crass." I take a physical step back as well, trying to distance myself from the swirl building in all the wrong places. The laugh that breaks loose isn't my normal one; it's too high and shaky. "I didn't mean for that to come out..."

Now it's her turn to suppress a smile, but dimples make a brief appearance.

"I used to be so damned smooth," I say and my hand runs through my hair.

She loses the battle and a grin surfaces. "Not always, Casanova."

"Fuck you," I growl, now terse from this inability to concentrate. I had thought seven weeks was a long time without sex. Try ten, almost eleven years, and now I was acting like a complete moron.

Her smile fades as my catalog of memories sweep through her mind. She straightens in the chair and her eyes widen. "You haven't been with anyone?"

"You haven't either."

"I had a child. I was a little busy."

"I was closing portals," I shrug, knowing it's not even in the same league, but I had to throw out some kind of excuse, even though it was bogus compared to hers.

We both just stare at each other and the chaos of pinks lacing through her aura makes me want to pull her over the counter into my arms.

"So, not even a hooker?" she asks.

Now I do laugh, and glance at the ceiling, formulating my come back, but all I do is shake my head. The sad truth is I didn't want anyone else, and sometimes a hand and a memory is all you need.

"And you didn't hide... anything from me?" she balks.

"No. You have everything." I tapped my temple. *At least everything that matters.*

Her gaze drops into her coffee.

"Do I need to look a little closer at your memories?"

The speed at which her eyes jump to mine tells me maybe I do, and I cock my head, offering a smile. Her cheeks bloom and her lips part as if she is going to speak.

I circle around the counter and she turns her chair facing me. The closer I get to her, the more pronounced her breathing is, and the more pink flashes in her aura. I slow, enjoying the pursuit and the flush in her cheeks.

Her hand lands on my chest and her elbow locks, holding me at a distance, but her palm against my bare skin burns in a way I missed.

"Bri," I whisper, and the plea is clear.

"I can't," she answers, slowly shaking her head. I cover her hand with mine, holding it in place.

"I came home for you." There's nothing like laying it all on the line in one phrase, especially when it sits out there like the last over-ripe banana of the bunch.

She pulls her hand out from under mine and turns the chair towards the counter.

I'm not sure what to do with her reaction. I'm a couple of steps away from her and I close in, putting my hands on the counter on either side of her.

"I saw everything, Bri. You can't hide from me," I whisper in her ear and nuzzle her neck. "And you know damned well I'm better than any of those toys in your nightstand drawer."

Her elbow rams into my stomach so hard it knocks the air out of me, and I stumble back. She spins towards me, swinging, and I catch her arm. When she swings the other, I grab it with my free hand. Her chest rises and falls, and the fire in her eyes sparks something deep within me.

Before I know what I'm doing, I have her pinned to the wall and my mouth is on hers, our tongues dancing in all the frantic anger and frustration of the past ten years. My fingers slide from her clasped wrists down her elevated arms until I'm cupping her breast in one hand and her cheek in the other.

The kiss torches everything inside of me, disintegrating time until her teeth bite down, drawing blood. I yank back and my hand goes to my mouth, coming away with red-tinged saliva on my fingers.

"You bit me?"

Bridget wipes her mouth, staring me down. "You cannot just take what you want."

I step back; every fiber of my being still tingles with her. Distancing myself, I take a few more steps back and run my hand down my face. It takes a few moments, but I realize just how wrong that was.

"You are right. I have no idea what..." I trail off and turn away. "I'm sorry."

"Jesus, Tom. What the hell is wrong with you?"

I let out a laugh. "What is wrong with me? Where do you want me to start?" I slide into the nearest chair and reach for my forgotten coffee.

The scrape of the chair next to me pulls my attention and Bridget settles into the seat, picking up her coffee again. She doesn't look at me; instead, she just nurses the coffee.

"I can't let you in if you're going to go off on another suicide mission," she finally says.

"I'm not going anywhere."

Her gaze rises, meeting mine. "Do you know how many gallons of angel blood the devil has consumed?"

Her left field comment makes me shrug. "What does that have to do with this?" I point between us.

"You're going to make a stand with your brother, aren't you?"

I lean back in the seat, away from her. "I don't have a choice. Not if I want to have a life."

"He's powered up, Tom. More so than what you hit in Death Valley." She taps her temple and her hand lands on the shoulder that kept me in physical therapy for months on end. "And he nearly killed you; imagine what he will be like at full strength?"

"He won't be at full strength. I have his grace and this is our turf. Mine and CJ's. It isn't a devil's gate."

She sighs and her hand falls off my arm and grasps her coffee cup. "I can't let you in." She shakes her head slowly.

She's trying to convince herself more than me.

"Hope is a powerful weapon, Bri," I say, and sip my lukewarm coffee.

She huffs at me. "I lost the luxury of hope the moment I gave birth to your daughter. Now, I have to be practical and think of her safety above everything else."

"So, the way we both feel doesn't matter?"

Her eyes narrow. "What is it you think you feel, Tom?"

"Love."

"That's just priceless," she leans back in the chair, slinging her arm over the back. "If you are so in love with me, tell me one thing?"

"What?"

"Why are you still wearing your wedding band?"

I look down at my left hand, at the wedding band my dead wife, Raven, had given me. From the moment she slipped it on my finger until now, I had never removed it from my left hand. She's been dead for almost eleven years, and it never crossed my mind to take it off.

"I just..." I have no idea what to say, and I have a feeling words would mean shit to Bridget right now. Instead, I slowly work it off and place it on the counter between us.

She stares at it and then brings her gaze to mine. A measure of shock is displayed in her irises, and in the slight part of her lips. I smile at her.

"You didn't think I'd do that for you," I say, and she slowly shakes her head. "When are you going to believe in me?"

Her eyes blink rapidly. "I believe in you."

It's my turn to laugh. "Yeah, like you were so convinced I'd talk to Damian about hiring you," I say, using a name I hadn't spoken of since I left.

"Well?" She cringes and looks away.

"And you don't think we can win this battle," I add.

She bites her lip, meeting my gaze. "Even without his grace, isn't he... supercharged like you and CJ?"

I open my mouth to answer and snap it closed. When Lucifer had his grace, he was supercharged beyond our combined powers, and on his own turf, he still had that spark, but I didn't know what kind of damage he could do on our turf without it. Michael certainly was more fragile without his, and he did not exhibit any psychic ability outside of Paradise Cove.

"I don't know what he's capable of without grace and outside the confines of a portal."

"Exactly my point."

I stare out the window at the ocean, weighing her remark. I know we are in for a nasty fight and there could very well be a line of casualties before it's all over. The likelihood I would be one is pretty high, considering what I harbor. Still, I can't help but latch onto that last sliver of hope. Hope kept me breathing, kept me moving for all these years.

"Do you love me?" I blurt, because while I feel it in her mind and her memories, I need the confirmation that this battle is worth the fight.

"What *I* feel does not matter. Don't you get that?" She slams her cup down on the counter and slides off the chair heading towards the front of the house.

I jump off my seat and follow her, grabbing her arm before she reaches the door.

"Bridget," I start, and she turns towards me.

"Don't, Tom. I saw what that bastard did to Hannah, and I saw the police report after your wife died. I know enough to scare the living shit out of me. I cannot..." She shakes her head. "...I will not put April in the same kind of danger."

"Do you love me?" I ask with more force.

Tears frame her lashes, and her jaw tightens. "Yes, goddamnit. I love you, you son of a bitch." She rips her arm from my grip and stomps out of the house with the slam of the front door.

Chapter 9

I STEP BACK INTO the kitchen after Bridget's hasty exit.

"You don't think Lucifer already knows you have another child?" Michael's voice startles me, and my gaze snaps to him.

"Excuse me?"

"If I was aware of your spawn, you can bet Lucifer will have already been apprised of that information as well."

Even his tone is condescending, and my fists curl at the need to punch the disgusted grimace right off his face.

He steps to the breakfast bar and bends out of view. When he straightens, he has a purse in his hand and looks beyond me. I glance over my shoulder, right into Bridget's wide eyes. I hadn't heard the front door open back up.

She sidesteps by me and crosses with all the attitude she left with, including a glare that matched mine.

"I would prefer if you didn't refer to my daughter as spawn," she snaps, and plucks her pocketbook out of Michael's hand.

"Do you know who I am?" he asks, puffing out his chest like a self-absorbed jackass.

She narrows her gaze. "You're the asshole Tom locked out of heaven."

I can't help the yelp of a laugh that escapes my lips and I cover my mouth. She hauls the strap over her shoulder and juts her chin out at Michael.

"I am the archangel Michael," he growls and pumps his chest up some more. "And you had better watch your tone."

She purses her lips at him but doesn't cower in the least. "You had better watch your tone with me." She flips her hair over her shoulder in a challenge, and then both hands find her waist.

It's the damnedest thing to watch, and I didn't think I could adore the woman anymore than I did when she walked out the door a few moments ago. But now, now, I need her on my side, backing me up.

"Tell me something, almighty archangel. Is Lucifer as impotent as you are?" She wiggles her fingers at him as she asks the question.

His hand moves to clasp her throat and stops an inch from her skin. Sam's growl overshadows Michael's and my hard warning glare makes him take a step back.

"My brother does not have the same limitations as I do," he says. "Especially with the amount of angel blood fueling him."

"Just as I thought," she spins on her heels and starts to leave.

"The safest place for you and your daughter is here," Michael says before she can march by me. I meet her gaze before she turns back to Michael.

"Why? So, we can live like fugitives? Hiding away until the devil walks in to kill us all?"

Michael blinks at her brazen response, and then raises his gaze to mine.

"He has a point," I say softly and look down into her hazel eyes. "If you and April are here, we can keep you safe."

"I don't need to be protected," she says.

"Your daughter does, and so does your friend Austin. They are the last of the angel blood outside of this compound." He points to the ground in front of him.

A chill swirls in my blood and I stare at him. "Already?"

"It made the international news." He hooks his thumb towards the dark television screen. "They were slaughtered."

The hourglass just turned, and the sands are sliding through at a pace I'm not sure either CJ or I are ready for. I turn my gaze to Bridget, sending a silent plea with my eyes.

"You can't watch us twenty-four-seven," Bridget says to me, ignoring Michael.

"Please." It's all I can drum up at the moment.

"The timing could be hours or days, depending on how Lucifer is traveling." Michael's narrative is irking me, and I send him a glare to shut the hell up.

"Michael's right," CJ says from the stairwell, pulling our gazes to him. "Hi, Bridget," he adds with a hint of a smile.

"Hey," she returns the salutation.

"I think it's time to assemble everyone on this side of the fence," he says. "Because otherwise, my brother will go off and do something devastatingly stupid to save you and April." He gives us both a soft smile, cocking his eyebrow, challenging me to say differently, but he's right.

"You and April can have the guest room upstairs and I'll stay on the couch in the basement."

"What about Paige and Austin?" Bridget asks.

"I believe Naomi has an extra guest room they can use until this is over." CJ says and looks to Michael. He gives a confirming nod.

I turn to Bridget and see the skepticism layered in her gaze and the tight set of her lips.

"Bri, having you here is better than having you vulnerable across town. I promise I'll give you your space."

"I can't just pull April from school. That's insane."

"She can join my home school program," CJ answers, knocking down another one of Bridget's arguments.

"You can make the choice. But he's right. You already know what I would do if Lucifer gets his hands on either you or April."

"Don't put that on me," she snaps.

"I can't survive another slaughtering of those I love."

"And you think I can?"

I keep eye contact with her. "You are stronger than I am."

"Bullshit," she hisses and takes her leave.

I follow her out onto the front walkway, catching up with her.

"Did you orchestrate that bullshit?" She points at the house, still moving towards her car.

"No. I didn't even know you were coming by." I grab her arm before she can open her car door. "Do not go."

She hesitates and looks at me.

"I can help you grab stuff from home and we can pick up April at school and bring her here. Please, this is the least I can do for the two of you." She rolls her eyes at me, and I continue, "When this is all over, I will honor whatever decision you make about having me in your life, but until then, for the love of God, let me keep you safe." Even I can hear the desperation in my plea, and Bridget sucks in her lower lip before she takes a deep breath.

"April does not know you are her father."

"I won't say a word. We can make up some bullshit excuse about the agency being a target, and we can say I came back to warn everyone. That could explain away my sudden appearance as well."

She cocked her head, narrowing her eyes at me. "You're pretty good at that," she says.

"At what?"

"Thinking up excuses on the fly."

I laugh and cross my arms against the chill in the morning air. "Yeah, well, my brain works on overdrive when I'm desperate."

"Ah," she says, and a smirk appears. "Are you planning on wearing that?"

I look down at my open flannel shirt and sweats and then back at her. "If it means you'll stay with us, I'll wear anything you want me to."

Her eyes sparkle with mischief. And I know I will live to regret those words, but I don't care. Even if she makes me put on a dress and high heels, it's worth it if she and my daughter are safe.

"Go put some jeans on. I'll wait here for you."

I smile and turn, jogging back inside while she waits by the car. My wardrobe choices are slim, and I grab one of the new pair of jeans I bought yesterday, buttoning and tucking in the shirt I already have on. I slide my bare feet into the pair of flip-flops I have at the top of my bag, instead of trying to find a matching pair of socks for the shoes.

Sam wags her tail as I lumber down the stairs. "Stay," I say to her, and you would have thought I just took away all her toys, but I didn't stop to reassure her. I kept my course, heading back outside. I close the front door and stop short.

The driveway is empty.

Frustration burns through me, and my stomach tightens. I turn, stepping back inside and CJ is already in the living room heading towards me.

"She gave you the shaft?"

I just nod, not trusting what my response will be.

He tosses me his keys and I look at them for a second, debating. Maybe Michael was wrong, but one glance in CJ's eyes and I know I have to either convince her or kidnap her.

"Thanks," I say and turn, heading after her, praying I don't have to do anything that will put a greater wedge between us, but deep down, I know her stubbornness is going to make that impossible.

I pull into the driveway of the office behind her car and shut the truck off, blocking her in place. I find her in the bedroom, haphazardly throwing clothes in an open suitcase on the bed, and I stand in the doorway, just watching her. The flurry in her mind is enough to make me clench the keys in my hand.

She turns with a handful of clothing and yelps at the sight of me.

"You can't run."

"Watch me," she says and throws the pile in her arms into the suitcase.

"Goddamnit, Bridget," I cross and turn her towards me. "You can't run from him. He will know you aren't here and he will find you and use you against me."

"You don't know that," she snaps.

"Don't make me control you," I warn and her brow creases.

"You wouldn't dare."

"I'm not playing games with your life. Or April's for that matter and I will be a fucking bastard if I have to be." I drop my hands from her arms. "So, take all the shots you want, but I'm not letting you go on a suicide mission." I use her words against her. "Not with my daughter riding shotgun."

"Fuck you!" She turns back towards the suitcase, trying to shovel the array of clothing into the confines of the box.

"I would rather you hate me than get hurt," I say and take a deep breath. "So, pack your bags with anything you think you might need, and then we are going to pick up April at school." As I speak, I push the command into her brain, and her mouth drops as her body obeys.

The glare she gives me tells me I've gone too far, but I don't care.

"I fight dirty, remember?" I say as she crosses in front of me and disappears into the bathroom, only to come back with her toiletries a moment later.

"I am going to make your life a living hell," she mutters under her breath as she packs the rest of her things.

Once she is done in her room, she picks up the empty suitcase and disappears into April's room. I close her bag and bring it down to the truck, tossing it in the bed before I head back to collect April's possessions.

She is nearly done with April's things, and I step close enough to reach out and tilt her chin towards me.

"I'm doing this to protect you."

She yanks her chin away from my grip and nearly throws the suitcase at me.

"Hey, I could have made you repeat the last time we were in your bedroom together," I say in my defense, and her jaw tightens, her eyes flashing a warning so deep that I look away. "So, I'm not that big of a dick."

She laughs and turns, leaving me with April's packed suitcase. I follow her downstairs and she disappears into the office while I put April's bag next to hers. Inside, I hear the scrape of metal against metal along with a stream of curses that should make me uncomfortable, but they pull my lips into a smile.

I step in the doorway and my smile fades as I stare into the barrel of her gun.

"I swear, if you don't release me, I'll blow your goddamned brains out."

"Put the gun away," I say with force, and she lets out a frustrated yell when the gun drops into a bag containing several other weapons.

"I hate you, Ryan," she hisses and the dark threads weaving through her aura, overriding what is left of the pink, supports her words, but I do not want to believe what I am seeing.

I kick the bag aside and step close. "No, you don't."

"Right now, I do!" She glares at me, and I reach out, gently pushing stray strands of her hair out of her face.

My touch brightens the pink strands in her aura, giving me that grain of hope that this could all be salvaged, with a great deal of groveling on my part. Instead of acknowledging her fury, I glance at the arsenal she's accumulated.

"I'm impressed," I say and crouch down, looking through the large bag. I pull a bow out and glance up at her, cocking an eyebrow.

"It's my hunting gear," she says. "I think your ass would make a fabulous target."

Even her sarcasm is cute, and I stow away the bow and zip up the bag. "You'll need to keep this locked up so the kids don't get into it," I say and haul the weapons over my shoulder. "You ready to pick up April?"

"No, but I have no choice, do I?"

"Unfortunately, you are correct." I open the door for her and lock up the house behind us. When I open the passenger side of the truck, she glares and climbs in. She would rather have her car, but that isn't going to happen. At least not until I can ensure she will not run away, as she was planning when I got here.

I drive to the school and park at the curb, helping her out of the truck before locking it.

"How am I supposed to explain you?" she asks as we walk to the door.

"Tell them I'm your bodyguard, because as of now, that's exactly what I am."

She glances sideways at me.

"I'll kill anything that tries to hurt you," I say in my best deadpan voice, and she slows, stopping just outside the door.

"You're serious."

I meet her stare. "I've never been more serious about anything in my life."

Instead of voicing any of the stream of thoughts flowing through her mind, she turns and enters the school without a word. I follow a few steps behind and hang in the doorway to the office instead of stepping completely inside.

Bridget adopts a pleasant voice and requests that April be sent to the office, making up an excuse of a dentist appointment. I'm surprised at the ease with which she applies the snow job, and I have a second to wonder if she's blowing smoke at me as well.

She glances over her shoulder at me and gives a small laugh, sharing comments with the school secretary. That same pink flows in miniature ribbons through her aura, and then it's gone almost as quickly as it comes.

Her aura flashes at the same time April steps out of the nurse's office with an ice pack over her eye.

"What the hell happened?" Bridget asks, waving at her daughter and addressing the school secretary.

"One of the boys hit her at recess," the secretary says. "He probably likes your daughter," she adds with a small smirk.

My protective instincts kick in, but I hold back. This is not the time or the place to make an issue of it. But as soon as we were under CJ's roof, not only would April start home schooling with CJ, she would also start learning Jujitsu, so if some other little punk tries to hurt her, she can take them down.

"Excuse me?" Bridget announces, loud enough to call the attention of everyone in the office. "Are you telling me it's okay that my daughter was hit because you think the boy might like her? What the hell kind of message is that?"

The school secretary's eyes bulge at Bridget's statement, but it is more because of her language than the real meaning of Bridget's words.

"I'm sure she didn't mean it to sound that way, because it is never okay to hit a girl for any reason,"

I say, interjecting myself before Bridget loses it completely. I can almost see steam rising from her. "And if she was insinuating that it was okay because the boy likes her, then perhaps she should take a hard look at the message she is conveying."

The secretary's attention is now on me, and her eyes are wide enough to see her entire irises.

I step to Bridget's side and place my hand on the small of her back, guiding her out with April's hand tightly in her grasp. We make it to the car before April takes off the ice pack and stares at me.

"Why are you here?"

"Because your mother needed a ride, and we are stopping at my brother's on the way home."

Her eyes darted to her mother.

"Uncle CJ's house," Bridget says and climbs in the front of the truck.

I open the back door and step to the side, letting April get inside. Silence prevails and I can't help but listen to the swirl of thoughts in both their heads.

"How much do you know about the business?" I ask, glancing at April in the rearview mirror.

"She knows nothing," Bridget says.

"Mom hunts ghosts," April says at the same time. "She's pretty badass."

"April!" Bridget turns, staring down her daughter with eyes wider than I expect.

"Yeah, I think she is, too," I say, and glance in the rearview mirror.

"You want to tell me what happened?" Bridget asks, still looking over the seat, bringing the conversation back to what possessed that boy to hit her.

April shakes her head.

"You can talk to me," Bridget says softly, and April meets her gaze.

"I told him about my dream, that everyone in York is going to die, and he got mad at me," she whispers, and I nearly run off the road. "York is going to burn," she adds after I jerk the car back into the lane.

It wasn't her words that catch me off guard; it was the vividness of the vision of my hometown looking like a battle zone that accosts me, and when I meet her gaze in the mirror, accusation leaps from her eyes.

"You're my father, aren't you?" she asks, changing the subject. I glance at Bridget, looking for help in answering the question.

"Why would you ask that?" Bridget's voice rises into that nervous tone that even April catches.

She glares at her mother. "I'm not stupid, Mom. I see the way you look at him and I see the way he looks at you. Besides, look at him. His eyes look exactly like mine."

That's a pretty astute observation for a ten-year-old, and I'm impressed. I glance back at her just before I turn onto Roaring Rock and nod. The kid has a right to know.

"Are you the reason I have these dreams?" she asks.

"I see ghosts, so I don't know."

Her eyebrows arch. "You see ghosts?"

I let out a soft laugh. "Yes. It's the whole reason I opened a paranormal investigation agency." We pull up to the closed gate and I type in the access number instead of just willing the gates open, like I could have done.

When I finally park the truck inside the garage and close the door, shutting us in, I pull the keys from the ignition.

"Why did you leave us?" April's voice is low and quiet and I glance at Bridget.

"I left so I could keep you safe," I say, keeping Bridget's gaze. The fact I didn't know I had a daughter until yesterday is a moot point. I turn away and climb out of the truck, opening the door for April and helping her down. When I haul the luggage out of the back, she stares at it and then me before turning to her mother.

"We are apparently staying here for a while," Bridget answers the unspoken question in her daughter's eyes.

"So, CJ is really my uncle and Alex, Amber, and Arianna are really my cousins?" There's an interesting spark in her eyes that makes me smile, and she smiles back. Everything clicks into place in her mind and she turns to her mother.

Bridget is sending me the evil eye, as if this conversation is not welcome right now, not with the danger that we all face.

"Yes," I say when she doesn't answer. "This is your family and right now, we are here to keep everyone safe."

"You brought the danger, didn't you?" she asks and I look straight at her.

"It would have come whether or not I was here, but at least with me here, you all have a fighting chance of surviving."

She steps closer to her mother, seeking comfort in the proximity.

"Go on inside," I nod to the door, and the three of us enter the chaotic family room. I leave them in the midst of everyone and haul their bags up to the guest room I had stayed in last night, dumping the suitcases on the bed. The arsenal stayed on my shoulder. Finding a safe place is going to be a challenge, but when I open the closet, a logical spot presents itself. The top shelf is half-empty and I haul the bag into the space.

Sam nudges me and I smile down at my ever-present dog.

"Hey, girl," I say as I step out of the closet and close the door. Squatting, I let her lick my face, and I rub behind both ears. "I'm sorry I had to leave you here, but it wouldn't have been a very fun trip for you."

I gather my things and carry my duffel bag downstairs, crossing through the animated discussions and dump my bag on the landing of the stairwell to the basement.

Instead of engaging in the heated discussions between Naomi, Michael, CJ, and Austin, I slide into the farthest seat at the breakfast bar, with Sam at my feet, and just watch. Paige sits with the kids on the couch, just as dumbfounded as the group.

Bridget doesn't know whether or not to interject and April just stares until she finally turns and trudges over to me, squatting to address my dog. She slides onto the seat next to me, watching with the same fascination as I am.

"You're not going to say anything?" she asks and turns towards me.

"No. Do you want a soda or something?" I ask, trying to be polite. Now that we are inside the confines of the house, I'm not sure what to do or say, and I've let go of the mental hold I have had on Bridget since we left her place. She crosses her arms, glaring at me.

"I'm okay," April says.

"There are some things you are going to learn in the next few days that are going to scare you. I'm here if you need to talk, okay?"

She looks up at me, chewing on her lip, and I study the bruise around her eye.

"Do you want more ice for that?"

Her hand flutters to the bruise, and she shakes her head. "I'll be okay. I didn't mean to upset Danny today."

"He shouldn't have hit you. No matter how upset a boy gets, it is never okay to hit a girl, and if anyone tries to sweep it under the rug like the boy hit you because he likes you, you tell them to go pound sand. It's never okay." I reach over and move her hair back so I can see the mark. "It's never okay," I say again and meet her gaze.

She looks down at the ground and I reach out, hooking my finger under her chin and force her to meet my gaze.

"It's not your fault, either. Don't even go down that road. A boy needs to treat his girl with love and respect, and not make her feel guilty for speaking her mind."

Bridget steps closer with her arms crossed and her lips tight. "A boy needs to learn to grovel when he's done something wrong," she adds, looking directly at me.

"I'm not apologizing for forcing you to come here," I snap at her at the same time the room gets quiet, so only my voice is heard. Everyone turns towards us, and heat fills my face. I certainly didn't want an audience for this argument.

"You forced my mother?" April's voice rises, and I look down at her.

"Yes, I did, because she was going to run away with you, right into the danger we are trying to avoid."

"Jesus, Tom," Bridget hisses.

"Everyone in this house has a right to know what's coming." The snarl in my voice makes both April and Bridget move back.

April's face blanches. "The dream..."

I meet her gaze, holding it, but I don't confirm or deny it. The fact my daughter is clairvoyant, and none of CJ's kids exhibit any supernatural abilities, tickles me, but being a dream seer probably won't bode well for her if Lucifer finds out.

I finally raise my gaze to Bridget. "Your mom has every right to be angry with me, but not about this," I say, and scan every face in the room until my gaze lands on Michael. "If I had been given the full set of instructions when I left ten years ago, we wouldn't be facing this sh…" I stop pressing my lips together. Shit storm isn't appropriate for some of the ears in the room. "So, if we are going to point fingers, we can all look to the archangel in the room."

I lean back in the seat and cross my arms. He glares at me, and the hate radiates from him in waves.

"We can play the blame game all day long, but it won't stop the fact that Lucifer is coming." Michael says, and he scans the faces in the room, including mine. "This house contains all that is left of the angel descendants. Lucifer would like nothing more than to crush most of you into oblivion, and the rest, well; you do not want to entertain the hell he has in store for you." His gaze lands on me to make his point.

April swings her eyes from Michael to me, her mind swims with what she is being told, and Bridget reaches out, placing her hand on her shoulder to lessen the building fear.

"We are angels?" she asks, and the shock of her words draws smiles from both CJ and I.

I shake my head. "No, the only actual angel in the room is Michael," I say, trying to bring her up to speed. "We are all grandchildren and distant great-grandchildren of angels," I add, to put some kind of reference on it that she can understand.

Alex sits on the couch with his arms around his sisters. "It's his fault," he says, nodding towards me.

"No. He made a valid point," Michael says, surprising the hell out of me. "He has made some very damning mistakes in the past, but this isn't one of them." He glances at CJ. "And he made a very recent decision that we never saw coming, but it may very well be the only choice that could end up saving everyone in this room." He turns back to me. "That was a smart decision, smarter than what I expected from you."

While I know it was a compliment, it was backhanded in a way that burned, but I keep the irritation to myself and just give a nod of acknowledgement.

"I think we've probably done enough scaring the crap out of the kids for now," I say, interrupting the direction of this conversation and sparing both CJ's kids and April from more of this dark talk. Naomi's children were teens and able to handle the uncertainty of it all much better than our kids. "Why don't you guys all go down and play some video games for a bit while we hash this out, okay?"

The relief on all the children's faces as they scatter and make a beeline for the basement makes me smile.

April remains in the seat, just looking at the group before she turned to me. "What did you do that upset everyone?"

I looked up at Bridget and she shook her head, her eyes warning me not to be honest with this one. However, the moment she is downstairs and asks the same question, she will be told exactly what kind of a monster I am.

"I killed my best friend to save my first daughter's life."

Her eyes widen, and she shrinks into Bridget's side. After a few blinks, she asks, "I have a sister?"

I shake my head. "No. She died, despite all my efforts to save her."

She turns to her mother. "Is that why you had me?"

Bridget's gaze rises to mine. "His little girl was not mine," she says. "I only knew her for a little while, but I was there for Tom after she died." She bites her lower lip and blinks, not knowing how to tell her daughter that she was actually an unintended mistake. She clears her throat and lowers her gaze. "Your father didn't know about you when he left," she says.

April stares at her mother and then looks at me. "You said you left to keep me safe."

My mouth pops open, and I'm not sure what to say now that I am caught in a white lie.

"He left to keep me safe, and by default, that kept you safe." Bridget saves me the pain of having to backtrack my words, but April's gaze hardens as she studies me. She glances between the two of us and slides off the chair, heading downstairs to be with the other kids.

"Way to go, asshole," Bridget mutters, and we focus on the rest of the group staring at us.

"She asked," I say, and defensiveness creeps into my voice.

"And you don't go telling a ten-year-old that she was a mistake," she snarls.

"I never said that." I put my hands up and back into the seat, trying to distance myself from her anger.

"You two can discuss your situation later," Michael interrupts. "We have more important things to discuss."

"Like, how do we stop York from burning?"

106

Every eye turns towards me, and a collective chill slips into the room.

Chapter 10

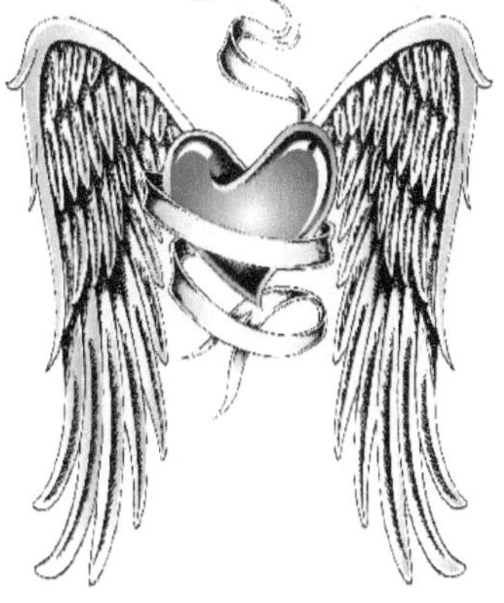

"WHEN SHIT GOES DOWN, the women and children need to get into the panic rooms we built," CJ says.

"Bullshit!" Naomi, Valerie, and Bridget say in unison.

"You built a panic room?" I ask.

CJ glances at me and nods. "Both Damian and I did, and it connects houses underground, so there is an escape route." His eyebrows stitch together. "You didn't know that?"

"No. I wasn't exactly paying attention that summer," I say and sigh.

"We did some serious revisions, like replacing the fence around both properties with bars that are a mixture of iron and platinum, and a solid salt line from rock wall to rock wall. No demons can get onto the property, and assuming there still are vampires left that Lucifer can call on, they can only access the property from the water. We basically protected this place like he had done to his property in Connecticut. Sigils, salt, platinum and anything else we could think of."

I really had been on a different planet during that time; I was more concerned with getting through the day after my wife's death than with anything else. I did nothing to protect our house, and I glanced at Paige and Austin sitting quietly on the couch, offering them a conciliatory shrug.

"We made sure the fencing around your place had the same protections," CJ says quietly. "Both Damian and I knew you weren't thinking straight that summer, and someone needed to watch out for you." His gaze moves to Bridget, and she sighs. Her hand lands on my arm.

I glance at her, but she is still holding CJ's gaze. I don't think she is fully aware that she reached out for me until my stare pulls her attention away from my brother. She glances at her hand and yanks it away, readjusting the expression on her face to annoyance.

Her aura threads with darker colors, and I can't tell if she's angry with me or herself. The silent pause directs my attention back to the family room.

"So, there's little to no weakness in the perimeter?"

CJ bites the side of his lip before he speaks. "I don't know. I only know how to defend against vampires and demons. There is no defense against crazy fuckers like the guy who killed Raven, and Lucifer can just walk onto the property, just like Michael did."

"And who knows what else Lucifer has at his disposal," I say, slumping in the seat.

CJ and Michael slowly nod at my assessment.

"This is such a fucking mess," I mumble, and swivel the chair towards the counter. Exhaustion from exercising control over Bridget, along with jet lag, seems to have caught up with me today, and I prop my head on my hand, attempting to keep my eyes open.

Bridget steps to my side and meets my gaze, with concern etched into the corners of her mouth and eyes. "Are you okay?"

"I'm tired," I admit.

"Go lay down," CJ says and I move my gaze to his without moving anything else.

"The kids are on my bed," I say.

"You look like shit," Bridget says, and I try to focus my eyes on hers, but my eyelids keep closing longer with each blink.

"This is what jet lag and exercising control over someone's will for more than a minute or two looks like," I mumble, and the throbbing in my temple fights to take over my entire consciousness.

"Come on," she says, and slings my arm over her shoulder.

I'm vaguely aware of her leading me through the family room, and the click of Sam's toenails as she follows us across the wood floor. Climbing the stairs taps me out, and when we get to the bedroom, she leans me against the wall while she clears the bed.

I hit the mattress and my vision fades behind the throb of a killer headache.

"Stay," I whisper, trying to focus on her.

She takes a seat on the edge of the bed and runs her fingers across my forehead and into my hair at the temple. The slow progression of her soft touch lulls my eyes closed and dulls the pounding in my head.

I open my eyes and focus on her for a moment. "I love you, Bri," I whisper. She rolls her eyes at me, but continues to rub my forehead and I let my eyes fall closed again, sinking into a migraine stupor.

"MR. RYAN?"

The soft voice reaches into the darkness, pulling me to the surface, and I shift, blinking my eyes open. April stands in the doorway with Sam licking her fingers.

"Mhm?" I mumble, and stretch. My head still has that post-migraine heaviness, but at least I don't feel like I have an axe planted in my cranium anymore.

"Mom asked me to wake you to tell you dinner's almost ready."

"Dinner?" I ask, pushing myself into a sitting position. Last I knew, it wasn't even ten in the morning.

"Yeah. You slept all day," she says.

"Holy cow," I whisper, and rub my face. "Did anyone feed Sam?" I ask, after dropping my hands to my lap.

April smiles and pats the dog on the head. "Yes. My mom did. We've been playing with her all day. She's a lot of fun."

I nod very slowly, taking care not to jolt my head. "You can call me Tom, you know," I say after getting my bearings. She just shrugs in that non-committal manner that tells me she still isn't sure about me yet. "Thanks for waking me. I'll be down in a couple of minutes."

She turns and Sam follows her downstairs. This is the first time since I bought her from that shelter that Sam has opted to follow someone other than me, and I can't help the smile that surfaces. It's as if the dog knows that April's safety is much more important to me than my own.

I head to the bathroom to relieve the pressure in my lower abdomen. After I take care of my body's needs, I brush my teeth and run my hands through my unruly hair, getting it back into some semblance of order.

It is much quieter downstairs now than when I was escorted to bed, and when I step around the corner, I see why. Only CJ's family and mine are sitting in the family room.

"Where's everyone else?" I ask, calling their collective attention to me.

"At Naomi's. We'll regroup tomorrow," CJ says.

"And Val?"

CJ's lips thin and he looks at his watch. "She should be here any minute. She had a few patients that she couldn't rearrange."

I can tell by his tone that he isn't happy that she isn't here, but I also get the sense he had no choice. Valerie was much more stubborn about her responsibilities as a pediatric surgeon than anyone else I know. That came first, even before her safety, and CJ seems to have accepted that over the years.

"Has anyone warned Steve?"

CJ stops what he is doing and looks at the phone. What color was in his face disappears, and both of us move at the same time. I get there first, pulling the receiver off the wall. I dial by memory, staring at my brother with my heart pounding in my throat.

After the third ring, the phone connects.

"I was wondering just how long it would take you."

The voice chills me to my core, and I meet CJ's gaze. Lucifer has Steve and Jennifer Williams, our adoptive parents, and I know damned well what he is going to demand for their lives. CJ's face echoes the same panic ripping through me, and I shake my head at him. We can't make the jump. If we do, we leave the possibility of Lucifer taking possession of either of us, and that would be a disaster for our family.

It's futile to beg for their lives and I squeeze the phone for a moment, gritting my teeth.

"You bastard," I whisper as I listen to the scraping of metal against stone.

"I want your brother's heart this time," he says with a laugh.

"That's never going to happen." I close my eyes, dipping my head because I know what the price for my insubordination is.

Lucifer locks onto my mind's eye, holding me hostage and giving me a full view of Steve and Jennifer in their apartment. I struggle to break free, but it is no use. And when he runs the edge of the blade down Jennifer's arm, she screams.

I bang my head against the wall, holding the ripping pain inside, helpless to look away from the unfolding massacre.

Steve bellows, struggling against the demons holding him in place. With whatever strength he has, he tosses the first demon on the ground and punches the second in the throat. His face is a mask of fury, the same type of fury pummeling every muscle in my body.

Just as he is within reach of Lucifer, that bastard snaps his head towards Steve, blasting him right off his feet. Steve sails through the sliding glass doors and right over the edge of the balcony. I can hear his cry fade and the faint sound of smashing metal, followed by the shrill sound of a car alarm.

"It seems your adopted father does not have the ability to fly," Lucifer says, and my knees buckle. The swirl of rage and remorse fills every fiber and I can't breathe. I slowly sink to the floor, still gripping the phone to my ear.

I know it's useless, but it still tumbles from my mouth anyway. "Please don't kill Jennifer."

The ghost now squatting next to my form overshadows the horrifying laugh that comes through the line. CJ throws a punch at the wall, burying his fist in the drywall.

The knife in Lucifer's hand lashes out, slicing through her abdomen. She screams as she tries to hold in her viscera. Blood spills along with her intestines and my stomach rolls.

He drills the knife into her multiple times, relishing her fading cries, and I just want the connection to end, to unsee what he is doing. The receiver drops from my hand and my breathing stalls and starts in inadequate fits until the light fades from Jennifer's eyes and the connection severs.

I can't seem to recover, to pull air into my lungs, and Steve's ghost whispers, "Breathe."

It's a mantra I've heard from his lips before, in that calming tone, that seems to loosen the tightness in my chest and give me the ability to draw sufficient air.

My gaze travels to Steve's ghost crouching next to me. "I'm so sorry," I whisper, and he pulls me into a hug.

"There was nothing either of you could do," he says, trying to wipe out the guilt embedded in my heart.

CJ is still beating the shit out of the wall because he knows as well as I do that Steve and Jennifer are dead, but at least I was able to block him from the disturbing mind-meld I had with Lucifer and the visions he fed to me. That is something I would keep on lock down until I stopped breathing.

Jennifer shimmers into view at the same time Valerie steps inside the house.

"Lucifer's in New York," I say, for the benefit of the rest of the family in the room.

Valerie looks at me, and then the spaces that the ghosts fill before her gaze darts to CJ and his bloodied fists and tear-stained face.

Tears don't come for me. They are locked with the horrors I've survived, and I stare at the ghosts in our midst. "You need to move on," I say, knowing what happens to ghosts that hang onto this life. My father was an exception and we all know it.

"Maybe I can help," Steve says, and I shake my head.

"Go see your daughters and give Hannah a kiss for me, okay?" My voice cracks and I press my lips together. My vision swims and I close my eyes. A hot path cascades down my skin and I swallow the lump in my throat.

When I open my eyes, Steve has his arm around Jennifer, and they both meet my gaze.

"We will see you again," he says, and I try to give them a smile. They don't know I've destroyed Paradise Cove and, with it, any chance of ever seeing them again.

"Go," I whisper, and they fade into nothing.

My chest squeezes and I glance at Valerie, still frozen just on this side of the garage door. Her complexion is ashen. My announcement of Lucifer and New York brings back all sorts of horrifying memories for her, and CJ's complete melt down doesn't help.

The hole in my soul widens again, and I finally turn my gaze to the family room, meeting Bridget's wide-eyed stare. The only other one staring at the spot Steve and Jennifer just vacated is my daughter, and from her expression, she knew them enough to be shattered by their death.

Valerie already has CJ in her arms, offering her warm comfort to her husband, while I shake uncontrollably on the floor a few feet away.

Sam whines, crawling across the floor. When she reaches me, she lays her head on my leg. She knows how close I am to losing my shit, and I look up at the ceiling, trying to control the whirlwind building in my chest.

It isn't until Bridget takes a knee next to me that I focus on something other than the swirl pattern on the ceiling. The words I said to her so long ago bubble up to the forefront of my mind.

"I should have let you run," I say. "You might have gotten far enough away to be safe." My voice is flat, devoid of the emotions tearing into my stomach, and I slowly stroke my dog to settle her. She's seen me like this enough to know there is a very dangerous storm brewing inside, but Bridget doesn't understand the complete absence of emotion.

"What is wrong with you?" she asks, tears flow in a steady stream down her cheeks and I stare at her.

"I'm broken," I say and find my feet. I need the chill of the evening air and the spray of the waves crashing on the rock, so I leave everyone and cross to the rock wall. I take a seat, stretching my legs out as I lean against one of the posts. Sam takes her position next to me and I continue stroking her head. The tide is rising and every now and then, a rogue wave hits the rocks and splashes up into my face, but I'm so numb that the cold does not penetrate my skin.

I don't acknowledge CJ when he takes a seat on the opposite side, adopting the same position. He is quiet, and I don't bother listening to his thoughts. I just need the nothingness right now, the numbness to remain and if I speak, the swirl inside me will crash down like a rogue wave and leave me decimated.

"I can't do this without you," he finally says, and I turn my eyes in his direction.

"I will not survive whatever goes down," I say.

"The hell you aren't!"

We both jerk at Bridget's harsh interruption. She looks at CJ. "Dinner is burned, and I think Valerie and the kids need you," she adds, and he glances at me. I nod towards the house, and he goes. I'm not ready for the turmoil inside the family room, and I look out over the ocean again.

"Sam, go inside." She points towards the house, but my dog doesn't move.

"Go take care of April," I say and she lifts her head, meeting my gaze for a moment before trotting off.

Bridget watches and then turns towards me. I turn away because I have to keep the shit locked inside right now. It's the only way I'll be able to function, and we've both seen what happens to me when I embrace the darkness. I end up under suicide watch in the hospital.

She steps closer. Her fingers touch the cheek facing the water, turning my gaze to hers. I meet her sad hazel eyes, and my teeth involuntarily clench. She keeps her hand on my cheek with her thumb caressing my skin. When the soft pad of her thumb travels over my lips, that flare of burning heat warms the chill in my bones enough for me to acknowledge her.

I shift, planting my feet on the grass, and pull her into a hug. My ear rests on her breasts and I focus on the thumping of her heart. She kisses the top of my head, wrapping me in her arms just as tightly as I hold her.

"I'm sorry for your loss," she whispers, and I pull away, meeting her gaze.

"I'm not the only one feeling the pain," I reply.

Her lip turns up on one side with acknowledgement. "I didn't think you were feeling anything."

I pull her closer, delivering a kiss. This is the only way I can show her what is brewing within my skin. It's the only way I can share my loss, and she gasps before she deepens the kiss, letting our tongues perform a slow and aching dance.

I'm the one who breaks the kiss this time, and I stare deeply into her haunted eyes. "He's just as dangerous as we are, except he has zero qualms about destroying everything in his path. CJ and I are hung up on preserving all we care about. That includes this town. The idea of innocent people dying…" I shake my head and press my forehead to her chest. "That's going to be the thing that undoes us."

Chapter 11

I DON'T KNOW HOW long we remain like this. All I know is the moment I let go of her, this connection will pass. Finally, I glance up. Bridget stares out at the ocean with a slow stream of tears running down her cheeks. I push her back a step and stand without losing the physical contact.

"If I come out of this alive, will you be there?"

Her gaze snaps from my chest to my eyes. Hesitation, along with a rollercoaster of emotions passes over her face.

"I might have to kick your ass first." Her voice trembles. "If you survive, will you be here?" She squeezes my arms.

"I'm not sure how much of me will be left, or if you'll even be willing to help me pick up the pieces," I say, searching her eyes and take her hand, covering my heart with it before moving mine to cover hers. "But if you are, then I'll be waiting right here."

She sucks in her lower lip and nods.

I inhale, centering myself and hardening my shell for a moment.

"Think you're ready to face everyone?" I ask and glance at the house behind her.

"I wasn't the one who ran off," she says, stepping back and wiping her face.

And like that, the connection breaks. I clear my throat. "Thank you," I say and drop my gaze to the ground.

"For what?"

"For reminding me what really matters." I step towards the house, and she follows. A new determination revives my senses and instead of the pain, I sharpen it into a boiling anger, keeping the lid on it until the right time.

"Lucifer must be stopped. No matter what." I glance at my daughter. "Even if it means the rest of this town burns." When I swing my gaze back to CJ, he stares at me with an open mouth.

"We can't..."

"We have to. That's his play. Devastate us and then strike in order to divide us. His end game still holds, CJ. He wants an army."

"You can't expect me to..."

I hold up my hand. "Do you want to win this?"

"Jesus, Tom, I can't let innocent people die!"

"Then say goodbye to your family, because that's who will suffer." I can't help the venom in my voice. CJ just blinks at me in utter incomprehension. "We have to think like Dad."

Our father was notorious for being ruthless when necessary. If his family was in danger, nothing was going to stop him from keeping them safe. Nothing. Not loss of life or limb or anything deterred the man. I never thought twice about that hard resolve of his, of that Angel of Death persona he displayed when cornered, but now I understand it more than I ever expected to.

CJ had yet to grasp it. Even though he could project the same image, he just doesn't understand the tenacity and dedication this cause requires.

His lips thin and his eyes turn icy. "I know what this requires," he starts, and I cross my arms, cocking my head in challenge. "But sacrificing innocent lives to protect our own is not okay. Ever. Just like killing your best friend to save your daughter."

He went there, and the burn starts in my core like a mini-cyclone. I cross the distance in seconds and slam him against the wall. There is nothing I can say because he's fucking right again.

"If we fuck this up..." I can't finish and he doesn't complete the sentence.

"You can't expect me to do nothing," he says.

"And you can't expect me to make those kinds of sacrifices. It's not in my DNA." We are nearly screaming at each other and the building tension between us is close to exploding. "This is a no-win situation, just like that phone call." I point to the phone. "The only way we win is if we take him on here." I point to the ground to make my point. "With all of us in the fight except those he covets most."

Horror dawns on his face.

"He's right," Valerie says from the other side of the kitchen. "We all have to be in this fight and with us here, there is no one for Lucifer to use as a pawn."

"You aren't fighting with me," CJ says, looking beyond me at Valerie.

"I will be fine."

"He snapped your fucking spine like a twig last time," he growls, and I drop my arm from across his chest, stepping back with as much surprise as that radiating from Valerie behind me. "I'm not going through that again."

His gaze narrows and jumps to mine. He turns and disappears into the living room and after a moment, the piano rings out as he smashes the keys, drilling out a tune that takes me a few seconds to get.

I step into the room and start laughing, crossing to the other side of the piano. I had never heard Highway to Hell so clearly on the ivory keys. He stops playing and just bangs his forehead on the keys.

"Raven was a pawn, CJ. So was Hannah. Lucifer tore me down to nothing and stole any hope of heaven in the process. I'm no longer pure in any sense of the word, in case you hadn't noticed, and I have that fucker's grace burning away whatever goodness is left."

He lifts his head and just stares at me.

"I don't think I could transfer the grace, even if I tried. It's bound with his blood inside me like a malignant disease." I inhale, calming the burn to a low simmer. "The risk in all this is that I fall into the same trap and have to make a choice. If that happens, you'd better be the one to rip my heart out, because if he gets his grace back, you are dead, along with Valerie and Alex."

He blinks his eyes and swallows hard. "I don't know if I can do that."

"If it comes down to it, you have to; otherwise, your daughters become the devil's concubines." Just the thought clenches my stomach, and I turn to step back in the kitchen, but Bridget's wide eyes meet mine.

I halt, meeting her glare.

"You said..."

"I said if I survive, I didn't make any promises," I whisper. "But I expect my brother to do as I ask if shit goes south. It's the only option we have, and it will save lives. Lives I give a damn about."

She studies me, and I keep her stark stare. I know it's not something either of us wants to come to fruition, but it's important to lay as much of the plan out there, so no one gets blindsided.

"How do we kill him?" she asks, looking between CJ and me.

I only have one idea of what needs to be done, and I glance at my brother before I answer. "We have to tear off his head." Visions of my father's head in Lucifer's grasp surface in an unwelcome wave, and I shiver under the thought.

"Tom? CJ?" Valerie's voice calls from the other room. We both cross and step into the kitchen.

"Where are the kids?" CJ asks looking around at the empty family room.

"I sent them downstairs when you took your argument in the other room. I'm glad I did. Look at this." She points at the breaking news tag on the television.

The screen displays the scene right out of a horror movie, and the caption reads Ex-FBI agent falls seventy stories to his death. Wife found brutally murdered in their apartment.

I glance at the clock. It had only been a little over an hour since that phone call, and the reporters were already swarming. When I glance back at the screen, my eyes widen at the image of me leaving the apartment with Sam by my side along with the tag—wanted for questioning.

"That fucker," I whisper and trade a glance with CJ. His jaw is just as tight as mine is.

"But..." Bridget starts just staring at the screen.

"He's framing me for their death," I say, pulling her attention away from the screen.

"But you were right here."

"Doesn't matter. He's hedging his bets, and after what happened to Jennifer, I'll be lucky if I ever see the light of day again."

CJ grabs my arm, turning me towards him.

"Lucifer gutted her," I say without sharing the visual.

"How do you know that?"

"He forced me to watch." I turn back to the television and the camera footage from the hallway outside the penthouse rolls across the screen again. The vision of me covered in blood is unsettling, but the additional touch of having an image of Sam next to him really burns.

I collect my thoughts and glance at CJ. "Why do you think I shut down like I did?" I ask softly.

CJ processes what I said with an open mouth, and he blinks a few times before he says, "What do you mean forced you?" He speaks slowly to control any chance of his stutter surfacing, and I let out a sarcastic laugh.

"I have his grace, CJ. We are inexplicably bound by the shit inside me."

"Damian wasn't," he points out, lifting a cocky eyebrow.

"Damian was not Lucifer's bloodline." At least that was my theory as to what was happening within me. Otherwise, I had no answer to how he could just lock me down like that, and force those images into my head.

The back door opens, and Michael and Naomi step inside. "Have you seen..." They trail off at the news report running across the television.

"What in God's name happened?" Naomi asks. Her voice, while carrying the pain of loss, also carries some accusation as well when her gaze lands on mine.

"Lucifer." CJ and I say at the same time.

"But that's you." Naomi points at the television.

"No, that's Lucifer wearing an image of me." I run my hands through my hair. "And if he continues to use my form, I am utterly screwed."

This new and morbid twist unsettles me more than the accusations being flung on the television. All I can think about is April's prediction that York will burn and if it does, that fucker will make sure everything points to me.

I turn to Michael. "He doesn't know," I say as all this processes. Lucifer wouldn't go to these kinds of lengths to set me up if he knew he had an ace right here in York.

A light of hope shines inside me, and I spin, staring at Bridget. "Lucifer does not know about April."

She glances from me to the television. "What does that have to do with him setting you up?"

"He wouldn't bother doing that if he knew he had some other leverage," I say and my heart rate increases with this new epiphany. My excitement is short-lived as the siren sounds outside the gate.

My smile fades and I move my gaze to Noami as every alarm inside me sounds.

"Panic room," I say, looking at her. "Now!"

No one moves.

"This is the beginning. Go!"

My voice barrels from my chest and seems to jumpstart the rest of the group. Both Michael and Naomi slip out the back, and I spin to Bridget and point towards the basement. "Go, keep her safe, please?" I whisper, and she gives me a shake of her head.

"Valerie, go with Bridget," CJ says, and she balks the same way Bridget does.

"No one has eaten," Valerie says.

"For Christ's sake," CJ says and turns towards the cabinet, pulling out a couple of boxes of granola bars, shoving them into her hand. "Just go."

After both of them retreat downstairs, I glance at CJ and he crosses to the call box.

"Hello?"

"Mr. Ryan? It's Duke Gallagher. Do you have a minute?"

CJ glances at me and I nod. It would make sense that the Chief of the York police department would be the one to notify next of kin.

"Sure," CJ says and opens the gate. When the police cruiser clears the iron, CJ closes it again. Duke is not alone, and neither CJ nor I recognize the deputy walking to the house with him.

Sam's low growl from behind me clues me in before CJ opens the door.

"The Chief is okay. I don't know about the other one," I say softly, and CJ nods. I pull Sam into the kitchen and give her the sign to sit. The television still drones behind me and I turn, willing it to turn off. Quiet emblazons the room and the front door creaks.

"Hi, Chief. What can I do for you?" CJ asks, with a steady and reasonable voice.

"I'm afraid we have some bad news. Do you mind if we come in?"

"Look, I don't mean to be rude, but I rarely let strangers into my house, even strangers in uniform," CJ says, in such a smooth manner I almost smile, but the fact he is leery of the other officer tells me he has no read on him, which is my problem as well.

"I'll wait by the car," the other man says. The door creaks, and footsteps enter the living room.

"I'm afraid there's been an accident in New York."

"I know," CJ says, and continues into the kitchen before turning.

"I need to ask..." Chief Gallagher stops in the doorway when his gaze lands on me. "...if you've seen your brother," he finishes with hardness in his voice that spells trouble. Just to prove he is in control, his hand lands on his revolver.

"Tom has been here for the last couple of days, sir."

"I came in three days ago and slept in what used to be my office that first night before I came here. I can get you my flight records and the name of the driver who dropped me off," I say to calm his wind up, but Chief Gallagher is still trying to reconcile the video he was shown with the current situation. His gaze narrows, especially when Sam whines at my side. I drop my hand to her head, calming her as best I can.

Gallagher glances at the clock and then back at me as a crease forms between his eyes. His time calculations of travel between New York City and York Beach, Maine, is the only reason he hasn't un-holstered his weapon.

"You also might want to pull my phone records. We called Steve's penthouse..." CJ's voice cracks, and he presses his lips together as his eyes close. He takes a moment to gather himself again. "We were on the line." He brings his glossy gaze back to the Chief's. "We heard firsthand."

"You'd better start explaining," he growls.

"The same... thing... that ordered my wife's death killed Steve and Jennifer." I cannot help the hostility in my voice, and his grip on the handle of his gun tightens.

"Son, I know you can do some hocus pocus magical stuff, but if you don't start explaining, I'm going to have to haul you down to the station until we sort out all of this shit."

"Will you trust me enough to step closer?" I ask, because if I cross right now, I'm likely to be shot and that would put as much of a crimp in our battle plans as me being hauled down to the station.

His lips pinch together and then he nods, crossing to within a few feet of me.

"You might want to be sitting for this," I say and irritation blooms in his eyes.

"Is everything okay, sir?" His radio squawks and he rolls his eyes.

"Yes. I'm just waiting for Mr. Ryan to get the last known address for us," he says, and it's my turn to cock my head. As soon as he finishes the transmission, he glares my way. "This better be good."

Relief floods through me for a second and I reach for his forehead. "Just don't shoot me, okay?" I ask, and he lets out a laugh.

"You would already have had lead in your ass if I was going to shoot," he explains.

"You might want to when you see everything," I say, and before CJ can stop me, my palm presses to his forehead. In order to show him enough for him to understand the danger we face, I have to go back fifteen years to the moment Damian and Naomi entered our lives. The flood I transmit includes both my thoughts and feelings along with CJ's. To understand, Gallagher needs to see heaven and hell, and everything in between, including what I did to Damian ten years ago.

As the last trauma of Steve's death passes through to Gallagher, his eyes clear and I remove my hand, stepping back, waiting for him to process.

Suddenly, he turns to CJ with his eyes blinking rapidly. "What. The. Hell?"

The scuffle near the back door pulls all our attention and Gallagher draws his weapon. The door slides open and Michael steps inside with the barrel of a gun pressed to his temple. The officer that had been with Gallagher follows him in the door with eyes blazing red.

Sam growls low. The deep sound rumbles across the room and I don't even look. I know she has her teeth bared and all the fur on the back of her neck is standing on end.

"Curt?" Gallagher asks, his voice full of doubt, even with the catalog of memories I shared.

"Curt's not home anymore," the demon says and his breath smells of brimstone.

"Well, shit," Gallagher breathes and takes careful aim.

CJ swats as if he's batting at a fly and the gun in the demon's hand goes flying right into my grip. Michael's roar jolts me and I am thankful I don't have a finger on the trigger and equally surprised that Gallagher has not taken a shot.

The crunching of bones echoes and Michael snaps the fool's neck, nearly severing the head from the demon's body. I guess he isn't as useless as I thought.

"Freeze," Gallagher announces, and Michael glares his way.

"Chief, that's the archangel Michael," I say under my breath, and he snaps his gaze to mine for a moment, but his aim doesn't move.

"I don't give a shit if he is God Almighty himself. He just killed a man."

"I killed a demon," Michael says with a mix of pride and wrath. His chest puffs in that way that I find condescending. "Would you have preferred I let him kill you instead?"

Finally, Gallagher lowers his gun a fraction and looks at me. "All that shit you fed me was real?"

I nod and the gun moves in my direction. Slowly, I place the service revolver I am holding onto the counter. "You get what's at stake, right?" I ask as I raise my palms to face him, but his mind was already flooding with my sins.

"You murdered Damian Andreas."

I bite my lower lip and nod. "Not my finest moment," I whisper after a beat of strained silence.

The gun never wavers. Neither does the hardness in Gallagher's eyes.

"You can arrest me after," I add, when he doesn't yield.

"After what?"

I glance up at the clock, calculating in the same manner as he had. We have a little over two hours before Lucifer sets foot in York and all hell breaks loose.

"After we send the devil back to where he belongs."

Chapter 12

IT TAKES CHIEF GALLAGHER a lot of convincing before he agrees not to arrest me on the spot. The fact that Michael adds to the conversation as a proponent of having me on the battlefield with him helps more than my brother's rationale.

When Chief Gallagher finally lays his pistol on the counter, he rubs his face. "You really know how to screw up someone's night."

I let out a sharp laugh. "Yeah, well, it's only going to get worse," I say, and glance at his hands. The wedding ring sobers me up. "Do you need to call anyone to tell them to get out of town before hellfire rains on us?"

He glances up at me and sighs, shaking his head before his gaze lands the same place I am looking. "Cancer got her," he says, and both CJ and I trade a glance. "How safe is that bunker of yours?" he asks CJ.

"As safe as we could make it. In layman's terms, it could withstand a missile," he answers, and Gallagher gives him a slow nod, both recalling vividly what a missile did to this very same property over a decade ago.

Chief Gallagher slips out his cell phone and climbs to his feet. "I need to let the police in New York know you have a concrete alibi, and we believe the video was tampered with."

I give him a nod of thanks and he steps into the family room with the phone to his ear.

"Are you serious about the panic room?" I ask, because I remember the amount of rubble that missile made.

He meets my gaze. "I think the only thing that could destroy it is angel fire." There is a clear warning in his tone that makes me inhale.

"Good to know," I say because who the hell knows what will happen when I confront Lucifer.

"You cannot lose control like you did at Paradise Cove," Michael says from his perch on the breakfast bar. He is nursing a black coffee like it's liquid gold.

"I'll do my best."

The cup slams onto the counter and his glare follows. "You will have to do better than that, because lately your best has been sorely lacking."

"Give him a break. He didn't have to go off and close the portals, but he did," CJ says coming to my defense.

Michael shoots him an equally damning stare. "I'm just laying it out for you. You've done some marginally redeeming things since your downfall, but I'm afraid it isn't enough."

"You know, I really don't give a shit whether or not I get into heaven. All I care about is making sure the rest of my family remains untouched. If I make it through the night, you and I can figure out a way to settle up." I stare Michael down, tired of his condescendence.

"Are you challenging me, boy?"

"You bet your ass," I reply, and he is on his feet in a blink.

CJ blocks him from coming around the island.

"Chill, okay? I've got bigger things to worry about than playing referee." The edge in his voice catches both of us and I put my hands up.

"Sorry, that was out of line," I say, trying to drop the tension a notch or two.

Michael's shoulders relax and his hands unclench before he gives me a curt nod.

"Can you bring some drinks and snacks downstairs?" CJ asks as he reaches for a tray over the refrigerator. "The natives are getting restless."

"Sure." I keep my initial response to myself. "Do they have facilities behind the vault door?" I'm half kidding, but when CJ nods, I raise a brow.

"They even have a mini-refrigerator and a microwave. We also put in a television and DVD player."

"And the only way in or out is through the house?"

When he hesitates, a chill tickles my neck. He opens his mouth and I shake my head, focusing on the Chief's thoughts as opposed to CJ's. If I have that kind of information and Lucifer somehow gets hold of me, the entire plan to protect CJ's girls will fail.

"I don't want to know. Lock it down."

Instead of responding, CJ busies himself with preparing a tray of goodies for everyone. When he is done, he hands me the overflowing tray and sends me downstairs. Sam follows and bounds forward with her tail wagging at the sight of Bridget and Valerie standing by the couch.

"Is everything okay?" Bridget asks.

I look between the two of them and take a long, slow breath.

"Yeah. Chief Gallagher has agreed to not haul my ass in until after the shit goes down with Lucifer." I place the tray on the coffee table.

"Why would he take you in? You have an alibi for what happened earlier."

"I have an alibi for that, but not for what happened to Damian."

Bridget's brow creased.

"I showed him everything that's happened since we met Damian and Naomi." I shrug. "So, I might not be locked up for what happened in New York, but what I showed him might be used as a full confession, and if he puts me in front of a microphone and asks the right questions, I could be looking at life in prison."

"You were not of sound mind," Bridget says softly.

I sigh and meet her gaze. "We'll cross that bridge if we get through tonight, okay?"

Valerie does not weigh in, and I glance in her direction. She drops her gaze, keeping her mind closed to me.

"Thanks for bringing the snacks," she says, and picks up the tray.

I glance around and can't recognize where the door to the bunker is, but neither Valerie nor Bridget go to leave.

"Where did you put my bag?" Bridget asks.

"It's up in the bedroom closet. Why?" I already know the answer. Her thoughts magnify the helplessness she feels, and that bag would give her a sense of security that playing a sitting duck doesn't.

"I want it," she says, and heads towards the stairs.

I give Valerie a tight smile and turn to follow Bridget.

"Stay safe, Tom," Valerie says.

I pause at the wall. "I'll keep CJ safe," I reply, glancing over my shoulder. "I promise," I add, and some of the worry lines carved in her face soften.

By the time I reach the guest bedroom, Bridget is at the opening to the closet. I reach past her and grab the duffel bag.

"I'm sorry," I whisper, and she turns towards me.

"Are you trying to sabotage any future we might have?"

I stare into her angry features, not knowing how to respond. Anything I say right now will set her off, and I am holding a bag full of weapons that could be used to make me regret the day I gave her a job.

When her lips thin, and her hands find her waist, I shake my head.

"No, but the Chief needed to know what is coming. Otherwise, he would have hauled me down to the station for who knows how long, which would have left everyone here vulnerable."

"Stop being so fucking honest, will you?"

Laughter chokes me, and she smiles at my snort.

"I'm serious."

"You want me to lie?"

"Yes. Well. No. You know what I mean," she says, and reaches for the bag.

As painfully aware as I am of time passing, I can't help but pursue this line of thought.

"I have no clue what you mean," I say, holding the bag just outside of her reach.

"Being honest is one thing, but baring your soul is another. Stop doing that with strangers."

I raise my eyebrows, surprised at the outburst. "You're upset because I shared my memories?"

She chews on her lip, staring at me, and finally nods.

"Why?"

"Because I thought I was special, but I guess I'm not." She glances at the floor.

I sigh, tilting my head to the side to capture her gaze. When she looks up at me, I say, "You are special."

She waves at the door with a huff.

"Memories and the emotional punch that goes with them are two separate things. You've seen both, even the deeper baggage that comes along with all the shit I've experienced. I have ever only shared that piece of me with you. Raven never saw that part of me, and neither has CJ. So, you'd better believe you're special."

The way her shoulders fall from the tight set of tension to almost relaxed releases some of the tightness in my stomach. Her cheeks flush and she starts that nervous shuffle of weight from one side to the other and back. When she reaches for the bag again, I pull it out of reach because I am enjoying seeing her humbled.

"Give me that," she hisses, and stomps her foot.

A genuine smile forms on my lips at her mini-hissy fit. Her hazel eyes flash with aggravation and an underlying humor that tugs at the edges of her frown.

"Give me a kiss and I'll give you the bag."

She balks, and I cock my head, challenging her. I know it's childish, but right now, I need as much to lighten the knot in the center of my chest as I can get, and teasing Bridget is providing me with a few moments of comic relief.

"Thomas Patrick!" she says, in nothing more than a whisper.

"Bridget Elizabeth!" I use the same exasperated tones she used.

Her fight not to smile fails and she pushes me against the wall, still trying to snag the handle of the bag. With a frustrated growl, she plants her lips on mine. It was meant to be a quick bribe to get the bag, but the spark between us ignites. My mouth opens, as does hers, and I thread my free hand into her hair, cradling her in place as the kiss sweetens with our leisurely tongue dance. My arm holding the bag lowers and Bridget's hand lands on mine and she deepens the kiss, increasing the intensity.

A loud bang separates us. I stare at her with my heart pounding in my throat and I am sure my eyes are just as wide as hers. Outside the front window, smoke rises into view and I hand her the bag.

"Go," I say, and she doesn't hesitate until we are at the top of the stairs.

"You'd better not get yourself killed," she says.

I give her a strained smile. "I love you, too. Now go."

I slide to a stop in the family room, making sure Bridget has safely disappeared down the basement steps before I turn to CJ, Michael, and Chief Gallagher, looking out the front window.

"We can't do this inside," I say as a certainty grips me. The entire house will implode if we choose this as our battleground. I can see enough damage outside already. The gate hangs open, adorned with twisted metal from whatever was used to blow it up.

I spin and tear outside with Sam at my heels and the first thing I notice is the stench of burning propane. I step far enough into the yard to see the

Long Sands shoreline, and my eyes close against the bright flickering of flame peppered throughout the horizon.

April's precognition of York burning was as accurate as it gets, and I shiver, glancing at the house just as a flow of demons come from both sides of the yard. Behind them saunters Lucifer, still wearing my image, including that cocky smile that usually melts women's hearts.

Sam positions herself right in front of me and every hair on her body stands, making her look just as vicious as her growl.

CJ and Michael step out of the house and stop. Their gaze jumps from me to Lucifer and back. I clench my teeth at Lucifer's perfect mimicry of my shaking fear. He is convincing enough that even CJ has a moment of pause. The hellhound adopting Sam's exact posture does not help.

Before I can signal CJ in some way, the demon horde Lucifer brought launches their attack. It isn't until I step into the fight that Michael heads for Lucifer, letting CJ and me take care of the demons.

Out of the corner of my eye, I catch a blur heading for Sam. I don't have a chance to react and her yelp as the hellhound's teeth dig in drives home desperation. My attempt at annihilating the demons with my mind only serves to push them off balance instead of turning them into dust.

When the first demon hits, I'm slammed into the ground with the force of his tackle. Air explodes from my lungs and I roll, falling back on my Jujitsu skills to throw the demon off. I no sooner get to my feet than two more attack, but this time I am ready, using everything our father and Steve taught us in self-defense.

The growling yanks my attention to the dogfight between us and I freeze at the image of the hellhound's jaws around Sam's throat. Her frantic eyes find mine as she tries to break the grip. Her paws rip at the hound's chest, but it's no use.

"No!" my cry sends a rumble through the ground like an earthquake, but I hold on to the angel fire burning my muscles. It's too raw and powerful, and uncontrollable for me to let it loose.

The hellhound shakes Sam like a rag doll and the sharp crack comes at the same moment I'm blindsided. From my stunned position on the ground, I see my loving, and ever faithful companion go limp. The loss hits like a lead weight, especially when her spirit peels from her dead body.

I break free from the demon pounding on me, and charge, diving and tackling the hellhound. A force I can't control races through my blood, painting my vision red. I wrap my arm around the beast's throat and squeeze, pulling its muzzle into the air. It drops Sam, but the damned thing keeps struggling, trying to break my hold. I pull with everything I have, bending its head back and twisting until its neck snaps, but that isn't good enough to satisfy the building rage. I keep twisting until the head tears clean off.

Hot hellhound blood saturates my shirt and jeans and I turn, pitching the head at Lucifer with a guttural roar. Instead of falling into defense mode, I go on the attack, pulling a demon out of the circle attacking CJ. Every muscle in my body is charged with fury and I spin, throwing the bastard into the two others charging towards me.

Again, I try to snuff them out with my mind, but all it does is make them stumble back a few steps.

The report of a gun makes me jump and I glance over my shoulder at the house. Butch Gallagher stands with his legs a little wider than hip distance apart and his gun trained on the surrounding melee. The second report echoes and another demon attacking CJ falls.

Before I can turn back towards those advancing on me, the Chief is launched backwards into the house by an invisible force. The crashing of furniture gives me a hint at the strength with which he was thrown, and I snap my gaze towards Lucifer. He has Michael in a mugger's hold, but before I can help, a couple of demons hit at once.

I glimpse CJ's split lip and bruised cheek as I break free and roll away from the demons. My roll isn't fast enough, and a boot connects with my lower back. Pain radiates from my kidney, but I force it out of my mind, climbing to my feet and throwing a punch of my own.

Air whistles and a breeze caresses my cheek. I spin in time to see an arrow embedded through the eye of the demon behind me, and he falls. Surprise rakes its nails down my back, and I turn towards the house as another arrow sails true, taking down one of the demons attacking my brother.

Bridget looks like a warrior princess in her tank top and jeans, with her hair pulled back. The rage in her features matches what pounds my insides, and when her aim turns towards Lucifer, the arrow falters at the image of me grappling with Michael. At that moment, a demon attacks her, and I sprint, avoiding another hit.

Bridget is driven through the open door and I can feel the angel fire surfacing along with the unbridled rage. A flash of metal flies through the air inside the house and the demon falls. I glimpse Valerie crawling from behind the counter and she gives me a thumbs up to tell me Bridget will be okay.

An arm wraps around my neck, pulling me away from the house and spinning me in front of another demon. The bastard smiles and his fist connects with my stomach, driving all the air out. I reach up and grab the arm holding me in place before the second hit lands. With a twist of my body and a hip roll, the demon holding me in place lands between us. I grab his head and twist with all the viciousness I can muster, and his neck snaps.

That leaves one demon between me and the group attacking CJ. Michael and Lucifer are still sparring, as if this is a demonstration instead of a fight to the death. Irritation burns and I refocus on the circling demon.

"Why the hell can't I just toast your ass?" I hiss through clenched teeth.

The demon smiles. "Angel blood," he says with a mouth full of crooked teeth. His voice reminds me of twisting metal and a chill slides down my spine. If angel blood hypes them up like a group of druggies on PCP, then I can't imagine how strong Lucifer is.

I draw in a breath, trying to center myself.

"Duck," Valerie's voice rings out.

I follow her order, expecting her knife to sail over me, but I'm not the only one who ducks, and when the shot rings over the backyard, I follow it, watching as it slices through CJ's shoulder, catapulting him over the rock wall.

Valerie's wail and two more rounds echo before metal clatters on concrete. Stunned into inaction, I glance over my shoulder in time to see her hair streaming out of sight towards the basement. I have a second to wonder where that extra escape route is before I am tackled by the remaining three demons.

Dozens of punches land before I can break free. I hold my arm against my pounding ribcage and cautiously move away towards the rock wall. The fact I can't feel CJ in my head brings a newly formed panic to my bones, and I glance toward Lucifer and Michael in time to see the final struggle.

Michael sways on his feet, hardly able to lift his arms in defense. Lucifer's next punch spins Michael, and he lands on his hands and knees, facing me.

Lucifer steps behind him and grabs a handful of his hair, pulling him back so I can see Michael's bruised face. His eyes lock on mine. Horror and defeat echo in his irises as Lucifer pulls out a knife. Lucifer waits with the blade on Michael's throat until I look up at his maniacal grin.

His eyes sparkle with bloodlust as the knife rakes across Michael's throat, slicing deep enough for blood to fly across the lawn in pulsing spurts. My stomach rolls as Lucifer grips his brother's head and twists it, decapitating Michael in one swift motion.

He rolls the head in my direction and points at me.

"Your turn," he growls as two of the demons grab my arms.

I spin, wrenching my wrist out of one demon's grip and land a throat punch with the momentum on the other. I mimic Lucifer and twist the fucker's head, snapping his neck before the two remaining demons attack.

An itch tickles my mind and I tap into my energy reserves, fending off as many punches as I can until I spin right into Lucifer's reach. His punch lifts me right off the ground, and the pain flares in my rib cage. I land on my knees and roll away before he can do the same thing he did to Michael.

CJ, if you're out there, I need you! I send the thought along with every ounce of panic pulsing in my veins.

I climb to my feet, taking stock as to where my attackers are. Keeping Lucifer in front of me, I slowly limp to my right, trying to keep my distance. I need to win. If I don't, my family will be tortured and killed until all that is left are the ones who can provide Lucifer with his army of dark trinities.

I need my odds to increase, and I sense one of the demons approaching behind me. I still have reserves left and when the crunch of the grass is close enough, I jump into a spin kick. My foot catches his jaw with enough force to snap his head almost all the way around, and the satisfying crunch of bone follows. I land, wincing as pain radiates from my ankle all the way up my leg. Not only did I kill the demon, but I broke my ankle in the process.

Fucking fantastic. I take a limping step and almost crumble, catching myself before I fall. The other demon drives in and the bottom of his boot slams into the calf of my good leg, just below the knee.

Ripping pain follows me to the ground and I roll, grabbing my knee as the howl escapes my lips. Awareness of a follow up kick coming in my direction splits through the pain and I roll out of the way, sweeping my leg, and dropping him to the ground. I'm not sure how I pull it off, but as the demon falls, he clocks his head on the edge of one of the rock pillars.

He doesn't get up and I force myself onto my feet because I am dead if I remain on the ground. My torn knee barely holds me, and I stumble closer to the house.

"Where do you think you're going?" Lucifer's growl precedes the yank of my hair and I fall backwards into him. His hand wraps around my neck, tightening enough for the airflow to shut down to a small wheeze.

"I promised you pain," he hisses in my ear.

I don't see it coming, but the searing pain across my abdomen reminds me of what that killer in Georgia used to do. My hands drop from the arm holding my throat to the hot pain gripping my stomach. Blood and entrails spill over my fingers and I gasp, trying to stuff my insides back where they belong. With his hand still clasped around my neck, holding me upright, he steps in front of me.

"That is only the beginning. I have a very special place for you in hell, and my staff has instructions to make your suffering more horrific than anything ever seen before." He smiles and his hand forms that familiar claw. "Now give me my fucking grace," he snarls.

His fingernails pierce my chest and I bellow in pain, even with the tight grip he has on my throat.

I'm coming, hold on! CJ's groggy and pain-filled voice fills my head.

I reach up, grabbing Lucifer's wrist, trying to stop his progression, but the blood makes my grip slick, and I cannot stop him. My heart squeezes under the pressure.

The whistle of air breaks my pain and an arrow pierces Lucifer's throat, shocking him enough to twist towards the house. His grip on my throat loosens and gravity does the rest. His claw dislodges from my chest as the second arrow pierces his chest and I land on the lawn on my back.

My gaze drops to the house as well, and Bridget sets up another arrow. Lucifer swats his hand as if he is knocking a gnat out of his face and Bridget flies backwards, right through the sliding glass door. The shattering glass cracks through the silence, and I grasp onto that last straw of anger.

I pool the power and shoot out what little angel fire I have left. All it does is pitch Lucifer ten feet onto his back. My failure magnifies as he rises to his feet, yanks the arrows out of his skin and then wipes himself off as if all he did was fall into a pile of dirt.

I shiver at the cold settling over me. My heart hurts, as does every other inch of my body. Heat fills my eyes and I say a small prayer asking God to deliver whatever CJ needs to beat this bastard. A buzz fills my ears, and the soft lick of Sam's tongue bathes my face. I look into her soft brown eyes and reach to pet her silky fur. My bloody hand touches air and falls back over my chest. Over my heart in the last protective action I can muster.

Lucifer is now in a dark haze, and he steps in my direction, but his head snaps to the right. White heat singes the lawn around me, and my battered brother launches at Lucifer. His golden wings are in full view, along with his blindingly scorching aura. The righteous fury emanating from him gives me a sliver of hope.

My body numbs and the thump of my heart slows as I watch the last battle unfold.

He has a knife. I send the thought just as Lucifer swipes it at CJ, but my brother parries like a pro, and with a quick maneuver, he disarms Lucifer. CJ controls his anger, using every bit to fuel his defense. When he turns the table and goes on the offence, his blows crack bone and split skin, until Lucifer falls to a knee.

That is the opening CJ has been waiting for and he grabs Lucifer's head, twisting with all the power of heaven behind him. Not only does angel fire add to his strength, it serves as purification, rolling across the blood drenched yard in a blinding light the moment he severs Lucifer's head.

The heat engulfs me, drowning out the screams of Bridget and my brother. My body feels light, as if it is rising off the ground, but my upward trajectory halts as Bridget reaches out, grabbing a handful of my shirt.

I meet her gaze and she yanks me down, trying to press me back inside my broken body.

"You are not dying on me," she says and Valerie blocks my view of her.

Warm lips touch my forehead and agony sears my soul. Blinding pain, flashes of light, and then it is all extinguished into the black.

Darkness drags me down, whether or not I want it to.

Chapter 13

THE BUZZING IN MY ears continue and I'm afraid to open my eyes, afraid of facing Lucifer in his domain. His promises were not lost in the transition, and cold bites into every layer of my soul.

The steady cadence of waves breaks through the buzz, along with the distinct sound of sobbing. I blink my eyelids open and my vision clouds. It takes me a minute to understand I'm not looking at fog, but drifts of smoke, and as the light wind shifts, stars peek out of the haze. The wind deepens the chill in my bones.

My focus shifts to the whispered prayers falling from Bridget's lips. Kneeling next to me, her hands are clasped in prayer, and her bow and arrows lay discarded to the side. A steady stream of tears flows down her cheeks from behind closed eyelids. I try to move my arm to wipe them, but it's just too heavy to budge, so I stare, helpless to offer any comfort.

My gaze moves a few paces beyond her to CJ and Valerie in a tight hug. My brother's back faces me, but his shoulders shake in the clear posture of grief. Chief Gallagher is on the phone asking the forensics staff to come along with the medical examiner.

A dull ache forms in my chest and within every inch of my body, and my lungs clench as if I have been underwater for far too long. That familiar burn grips me and I force an inhalation. The cold air tingles as it fills my oxygen-starved lungs.

My first attempt at speech is only a soft wheeze, and I close my eyes, gathering my strength.

"Who died?" I say loud enough to draw attention, but my voice sounds like I swallowed a shovel full of gravel.

Bridget's eyes snap wide enough for me to think they might just shoot right out of her head. CJ spins out of Valerie's arms, facing me with tear-soaked cheeks. His eyes are just as wide as Bridget's.

"And send an ambulance," Chief Gallagher says into the phone before he ends the call.

They all gather around me as if they are witnessing a miracle.

"You did," CJ says, and his voice is raw from the kind of crying tied to grief. I should know. I'm the king of emotional disasters.

I turn my head, look at the bodies still strewn across the lawn, and then turn back to Bridget, Valerie, and CJ. Valerie squats and takes my wrist, with lips pressed together in doubt. After a minute, her eyes widen, and she glances up at CJ.

"He has a pulse, but it's weak," she says and then drops her gaze to me.

"I was dead?" I'm still trying to catch up with the conversation.

Bridget still hasn't moved, and her face is now paler than it was before. Her gaze drifts down my body and back, as if she does not trust what she is seeing and hearing.

"My healing mojo didn't fix everything," she says. "You had lost too much blood..." She trails off and closes her eyes, putting the back of her wrist to her forehead. Her hand is covered in blood. "I tried CPR, but..." She blinks her eyes and a tear rolls down her cheek.

I move my gaze to the starry heavens above and then turn to Bridget as a memory surfaces. "You were the one who caught my spirit," I say.

She finally nods, but it is very slow, cautious, and her gaze jumps to my dead doppelganger a few feet away.

"How are you alive?" she asks, and she is the only one who has fear quaking her voice. "You were dead, like, no pulse, no breathing, dead. For at least five full minutes before Valerie stopped trying to revive you, dead."

I really want to say 'sometimes we come back', but the fear radiating from her is enough to chill out my warped sense of humor. CJ's smirk tells me he's in my head, but he has the courtesy of not repeating my thoughts. That familiar connection settles my nerves.

My fingers tingle and I wiggle them back to life, focusing on Bridget and her nearly hysterical question. She's on the edge and I want to reach out to her, but I have a feeling she would freak out more than she already is. I move my shoulders in a shrug because I have no explanation, especially since Valerie said her healing powers were useless.

"It might have been Raphael's grace," CJ says and I meet his gaze. "I had to try something. I wasn't ready to let you go." He looks up at the sky, blinking. When he seems to have his shit together, he continues. "Uriel's grace brought Valerie back, so I figured my best bet was giving you the grace of your great grandfather." He presses his lips together. "It didn't take right away, either," he adds, swiping at his eyes as he glances out over the ocean. "Needless to say, I didn't take it too well, so... you might have a broken rib or two." He gives me that cockeyed smile and I let out a soft laugh.

"I can deal with broken ribs," I say to the clouds above me.

"You are still in rough shape," Valerie says.

I turn to her before following her gaze to my chest. It's covered with thick, tacky blood, imprinted with her palm print where she tried chest compressions to revive me. Blood oozes from the welts where Lucifer's nails had sunk into my skin. I look beyond my chest, expecting to see my abdomen sliced open, but no scar remains where Lucifer gutted me.

I push up on my elbows and wince with pain as my midsection screams at me. My muscles still feel like they had been run through a woodchipper, but I force myself to focus and rotate my right ankle, bracing for pain that never comes. I lower my head back to the ground and pull my feet in, raising my knees, thankful that the last of the damage from what the demons did no longer exist. I sigh, thankful for small victories, but based on how I feel now that the numbness is receding, I have a feeling I might be in for more than just outpatient services.

"You are probably going to need a transfusion," Valerie says.

I nod and refocus on Bridget. Now that I can move, I reach out and take her hand, studying her. "Valerie fixed you up, too?"

She gives a little laugh and a nod. "The glass cut me up pretty badly."

Chief Gallagher steps into view and squats, running a hand down his face. "I have no idea how I am going to explain all this." He glances around at the carnage and shakes his head. "But I'll figure out a way."

I give him a small nod. Any more than that makes my stomach clench and the world spin. My eyes slip closed and Bridget's grip on my hand tightens, snapping my lids back open. I look at the fear carved in her face.

"I'm not dying again," I whisper. "I'm just in a hell of a lot of pain." I squeeze her hand gently, and her lips stretch into what she hopes is a smile, but all I see is a grimace. I try on a smile of my own. "I promise."

"Mom!" April's shrill cry rings from the house.

"She shouldn't see this," I say, but the girl is already running across the yard, dodging the dead bodies, followed by CJ's kids.

She skids to a stop next to Bridget at the same time CJ's kids fall into Valerie's and CJ's arms. Behind them, Naomi and her children follow slower, scanning the carnage as their faces go pale, and in the rear come Austin and Paige, looking as shell-shocked as I am sure everyone else is.

The slow realization that the people we have been tasked with protecting for the past fifteen years would never need our services again crawls into my mind, and I trade a glance with CJ. He presses his lips together and nods. While we both mourn the loss of Steve and Jennifer, and a hole in

my chest remains for Sam, I can't help but embrace
the hope filling my senses.

Chapter 14

HOSPITAL FOOD SUCKS AND I pick at the green gelatin as the electrocardiogram beeps in a semi-steady rhythm. My diagnosis is six cracked ribs, along with myocardial contusion. A bruised heart, which means I am sequestered in a hospital bed until my heart rhythm returns to normal.

My red cell count is low as well, but I can't exactly tell them I already bled out on my brother's backyard, so I succumb to a transfusion along with a healthy dose of pain medicine and every conceivable test known to man. I have been poked and prodded, stuck and scanned for the last few hours, and they finally left me hooked to the ECG and two separate intravenous bags, one with blood, the other with saline and those horribly mind-bending pain meds.

Valerie and CJ step into the room once the doctor steps out. I glance up from the tray, rolling my eyes. Both of them are clean, and that old twinge of jealousy hits. While they cleaned most of the blood and gore from me prior to patching up my chest, I still had streaks of it on my skin.

"At least twenty-four hours on this monitor?" I say, hooking my thumb at the beeping machine. My voice sounds distorted in my ears and annoyance blooms at the medicine impeding my speech.

Valerie steps closer and leans in, pressing her lips to my cheek. A tingle starts in my ribs and then the blinding pain grips me, making my heart, and the monitor, beat more erratically.

"Shit, woman, a little warning," I hiss as my ribs mend under her healing magic. At least the pain is dulled by the medicine they are pumping into me, but it is still bad enough to register in my fog-filled brain.

"I doubt it will fix your heart, but it should fix the damage CJ and I did to your ribs."

"You mean *you* crushed my ribs?" I ask, because I saw the x-ray and it wasn't pretty, but at least they didn't need to crack me open to fix the damage.

She gives me a tilted smile. "I'm responsible for the crack in your sternum."

A nurse comes darting in before I can say something rude to Valerie about finally doling out a little justice of her own. Her tilted smile grows, and she sends me a wink while the nurse dotes on me.

Concern presses the nurse's lips in a straight line, and her gaze bounces from the monitor to me.

"I'm fine, I just shifted my weight," I say, trying to give a logical explanation, but she comes to the side of the bed, crowding Valerie and CJ out of the way.

"Perhaps you should rest," she says and picks up my wrist.

"What I'd really like is a shower and something clean to wear," I mumble, and she gives me the same look she did when they first rolled me into this room.

"Tomorrow, Mr. Ryan," she reminds me, and I nod. She turns to CJ and Valerie. "Perhaps you should let your brother get some rest."

"I said I am fine."

CJ and Valerie exchange a glance before they look at me. "Get some rest. We'll bring you some clean clothes in the morning," CJ says and leads Valerie out the door.

The nurse follows them out and lowers the lights, drenching me in darkness.

I lie back on the bed and my gaze travels to the window and the night beyond. As much as I'd like to rest, I'm not sure what form of nightmare will grip me as soon as I fall asleep.

The door squeaks, and I turn my head. The soundless movement across the dark room gives me a start, but the moment the weight gathers on the edge of the bed, I stiffen.

"Bri?" It's the only logical explanation.

"Yeah," she whispers and I shift, giving her more room than just the half inch between the edge and me.

"Come here," I say in a low whisper, and she doesn't hesitate. She slides to my side, stretching out next to me, and her head finds my shoulder. My arms wrap around her as best as I can, but I'm limited with all the wires and tubes. Still, having her against me strengthens my heartbeat, steadying me. I press my lips to her forehead. "Where's April?"

"She's having a girl's night with Grace at Naomi's."

"And you didn't want some of that fun?"

She laughs softly. "No. I needed... this." She gives me a gentle squeeze.

It isn't until the bed shakes that I realize she's crying. I can't see her face in the dark, but the damp heat where her cheek rests on my shoulder is enough.

"Babe, please don't cry," I whisper, and gently run my fingers through her hair.

"You were..." Her voice chokes on the sob and I pull her to my lips, quieting her and trading memories, so she doesn't have to tell me how much my death crushed her.

When the kiss breaks, my eyes burn with unshed tears. The turmoil still present within her tempers my horror at what I saw through her eyes. I knew I had been bad off, but I had no idea just how close Lucifer had been to getting his grace and damning my soul to hell forever.

"I'm so sorry," I whisper in her ear.

"I haven't prayed that hard for a miracle in years," she sniffles.

"I'm glad someone upstairs heard you," I say, and she squeezes me tighter. I let out a soft laugh. "I'm afraid to go to sleep," I admit, and her head lifts off my shoulder.

"Why?"

The burn in my eyes increases and I blink, trying to soothe it. Hot paths trace down into my ears and the memory of my father's disorientation when we pulled him out of hell lingers. "What if this isn't real? What if I wake up to find I have utterly failed, and I'm in the pit?"

Her hand finds my cheek and her gentle caress grounds me, but that nagging fear keeps me on edge.

"What if I can't ever get rid of this fear?" I ask, but it isn't for Bridget to answer. It's for me to deal with, and I squeeze her tighter to me. If this is a dream and I'm indeed in hell, I'm holding onto this vision as long as I can.

Chapter 15

AT SOME POINT DURING the early hours of the morning, the medicine and exhaustion won out. I slept dreamlessly and soundly, with Bridget tucked by my side. My eyes blink open to the bright sunshine filtering into the room and I turn my head, expecting Bridget still to be next to me, but the bed is empty. My heart trips and the monitor echoes the change in adrenaline.

A light sweat breaks out on my exposed skin, and my breathing picks up as well. My eyes dart from corner to corner, looking for signs I might be missing. When my heart rate pulses in my temple, the door opens, and a nurse rushes in.

"Where is she?" I ask, my voice hoarse from sleep.

"Mr. Ryan, I suggest you calm down," she says softly, her wide eyes dart to the display and then back to mine.

"She was here when I went to sleep," I say as I try to calm my breathing, but my pulse continues to race.

"Who?" the nurse asks and checks my IV line. After a moment, the burn of medicine filters into my vein, and I glare at her.

"I don't need drugs," I say, even as the edge seems to come off the panic gripping me.

She pats my hand. "You've been through quite the trauma, sir. It's normal to have some disorientation." She glances at the chart and then up at the nearly empty bags of blood. She smiles and leans over, unplugging the drip from my hand before pulling the empty bags from the post. She drops them in the hazard box and returns to my side.

The anxiety still resides at my core, but my attention focuses on the nurse removing the blood transfusion tube from my hand. "But Bridget was here with me last night. Where is she?" I ask again after she presses a band-aid over the entry point.

Before she can answer, the door opens and all the tension releases at the sight of Bridget carrying two Dunkin Donuts coffee cups. Her smile fades and a crease appears between her eyes as she meets my gaze.

The nurse turns. "Visiting hours aren't for another hour."

"She can stay," I say and the nurse glances at me, raising an eyebrow in a challenge.

My gaze hardens. "Bridget can stay," I insist, pushing the command and the nurse purses her lips, but doesn't contradict the command. She gives Bridget a glare as she leaves the room.

"I thought you might need some coffee today," she says and puts the cup on the table next to me.

I glance at it. "I'm not sure I'm allowed yet," I say and give her a smile. I don't want her to know how panicked I got when I woke up and she wasn't here, but I guess I don't do a very good job of it.

"You were freaked out," she says and leans back in the chair.

I let a little laugh escape. "No," I add, but she knows. In the light of day, all my fears seem to be unwarranted, and I grab the coffee off the table. Rules be damned.

"How are you feeling?"

I take a sip of the coffee and close my eyes, debating on how to answer. My chest still aches, as does every muscle in my body, but there is no pain. "I'm not bad," I say after my self-assessment. "Considering I still smell like death," I add, and open my eyes.

"Well, now you smell like death and coffee," she smiles and glances at her phone. "CJ said the cops were still trying to figure out what in the hell happened and what those things were in the yard." She glances up at me. "Apparently, neither Michael nor Lucifer had a heart. It has completely freaked out the medical examiner. And no one can identify what kind of animal attacked your dog."

My smile fades at the mention of Sam. I'm not sure the mystery of the hellhound will be solved, but the ache in my chest gets worse. "She was such a great dog," I say and glance out the window.

Her hand touches mine, and I glance at the contact.

"What happened to keeping your distance?" I ask and thread my fingers through hers.

Her cheeks flush and she looks at the ground. "You came back," she whispers and shrugs.

"I'm still damaged," I gently remind her, but keep her hand in mine.

"I'm not exactly a pillar of strength, either," she says, and I laugh.

"You could have fooled me. You were fearless and pretty damned accurate with those arrows."

She meets my gaze, but there is no smile. "I knew what was at stake if we lost."

That nonchalant shoulder shrug appears, minimizing her contribution to the fight, and I was having none of it. "You were the one who saved us. If you hadn't created a diversion..." I close my eyes and take a deep inhalation, trying to loosen the knot that built as we discussed what could have happened. "You saved all our asses."

"CJ did that."

I shake my head and meet her unsure stare. "CJ ended the threat, but you gave him the time he needed to get it done." I took another sip of coffee and sighed, running my hand down my face. "He got shot, and I never asked him how he was doing." I exhale.

"I'm fine, but for a while there, I wasn't so sure. It's a miracle I didn't bash my head on any of those rocks. As it was, I broke my hip when I fell, and halfway to the dock, I blacked out. That's why it took me so goddamned long to get my ass up the ladder and back in the game," CJ says, stepping into the room. "I guess we are both damned lucky it was high tide."

I had no idea how bad off he had been, but it explains the lack of mental connection for part of the time I fought those bastards. I give him a nod of acknowledgement.

He smiles at me. "The yard is a fucking mess. I didn't realize demon blood was black and as hard to get rid of as melted tar."

"What are you talking about?" I clearly remember him blowing up a couple of demons and what went splat was red.

"None of the demons we ever fought before this were Lucifer's guards," he says softly. "And I think we're going to have to dig up the entire backyard and reseed."

Such mundane and utterly normal stuff to worry about pulls a smile to my face. "It's nice for that to be your biggest worry," I say and he huffs a laugh.

"Yeah, well, I'm sure when my daughters start dating, I'll be a fucking basket case, especially knowing there are guys like you out there."

Bridget chuckles and glances at him. I press my lips together against the smile gaining traction, but both CJ's etched dimples and Bridget's laugh make me lose the battle.

"I don't think I'll be any different," I say and tighten my grip on Bridget's hand just in case she decides this is the moment to pull away and protect her heart.

She squeezes back.

The nurse steps into the room, and a crease appears between her eyes as her lips thin. "Visiting hours are not for another half an hour."

"Come on, Mary, you know Tom's my brother," he says, rolling his eyes at her. I didn't realize he knew the nurses by name, but I guess with Valerie's connections, he probably knew most of the hospital staff by first name.

"Do I have to call your wife?" Her arms cross.

CJ does that puppy-dog eyes thing. "Can't you just bend the rules for today? I'm already here, besides I brought him some clothes," he says, holding up my duffel bag, and gives her that signature smile I have seen on television more than a dozen times over the years. It always causes a collective sigh from the female audience and this situation is no different.

She makes that sigh and comes to my side, breaks the grip I have with Bridget, and checks my pulse. She glances at the coffee in my free hand and plucks it out of my hand.

"No caffeine until the doctor reviews your results."

I balk, but don't say a thing. We are already pushing our luck at this point, and I'd rather have Bridget and CJ here than a coffee, anyway. Instead, I ask, "Can I take a shower and put on some real clothes?"

"As soon as the doctor looks at you," she says. "He should be in here within the next half hour."

"Okay," I say, dropping my gaze. The need to feel clean is becoming as dominant as my need for food, and my stomach growls in response.

She pulls out a small vial syringe and attaches it to the open port in my IV, decompressing the handle until the vial is full. "Just checking your blood count," she says when she unclips it and then she disappears out of the room.

I glance back at CJ and Bridget.

"I really want to get the hell out of here."

CJ's expression sobers up, and he glances out the window. "Valerie explained the seriousness of your heart injury." He shifts and looks at the floor before meeting my gaze again. "You need to make sure your heart is as close to normal as possible before you check yourself out of here."

I bite my lip, trying to read into his mind, but he's blocking me.

Bridget turns and stares at CJ. "Why?"

"He could have a heart attack if he's not careful. That's why they are dancing around his aggravation and sedating him when he gets too... excited." CJ looks from Bridget to me. "You aren't out of danger yet." His hands slide into his pockets. "And Valerie's magic can't fix it."

The seriousness in both his features and his tone makes me nod slowly.

"So, if I push my luck, my ticker gives out?" My hand rises to cover my heart and I flinch at the pressure against the cuts underneath.

"Pretty much," he says.

"For how long?" I glance at Bridget for a moment before I meet CJ's gaze. He just shrugs.

"I'm not a doctor," he says.

"This isn't... permanent?" The monitor echoes the increase in my heart rate at the idea of being limited for the rest of my life, in ways I can only imagine.

Again, that fucking shrug. Before I can get any more uncomfortable with this conversation, the doctor waltzes in.

He is studying his tablet, swiping from screen to screen before he takes a seat on the rolling chair. He rolls to the ECG output as we all watch him. His mental narration is too clinical for me, so I glance at CJ. He gives me the *'I have no fucking clue'* shrug.

The doctor whistles, and my heart leaps into my throat. The auditory trigger catapults me back to the carving table in Georgia and terror grips every cell. My hands tighten on the rails of the bed as the pain spirals from my heart outward.

The whistling stops and he jerks his head towards me as the ECG goes haywire. He didn't quite understand why his whistling knocked me into cardiac arrest, but my frightened stare meets CJ's and the sound in the room fades to a high-pitched buzz.

I'm spinning, and my chest feels like someone just punched through it. I wonder if this is what Damian felt when I blew up his ribcage. My vision tunnels, darkening at the edges.

"You promised me!" Bridget's scream breaks through and my gaze snaps to hers.

"I'm not going anywhere." I try to speak, but I can't, so I send the thought to her as CJ grabs her and drags her from the room.

It takes me a minute to realize I am not observing the room from the bed, from my wide-open and unfocused eyes.

Shit.

I am not in my body and that high-pitched buzz is the heart monitor flat lining.

I promised Bridget I wouldn't die, and here I am, breaking her heart yet again.

"This is not happening," I say, willing my spirit to meld with my skin.

When nothing happens, aggravation flushes my vision. "Goddamnit! Do something!" I yell at the roomful of doctors.

"Clear!"

The electricity buzzes through my body and my viewpoint changes with the jolt. The doctor holding the paddles goes flying across the room, and I sit up, feeling every ounce of Raphael's angel grace melding inside me. It's just as painful as absorbing Lucifer's grace was, but this comes with an agonizing side benefit, the mending of my heart. I curl into a ball as light pours from me, blinding everyone in the room, and I don't realize I'm bellowing through the suffering until both the light, and my voice, fade.

I pant, scanning the shocked group of doctors and nurses, wondering why this didn't happen on the battlefield when CJ pushed the grace inside me.

My gaze stops at the open doorway and both CJ and Bridget standing with open mouths. Everyone is staring at me with open mouths.

"You could catch flies with that," I say to my brother, resurrecting one of our mother's lines from when we were little. His mouth pops closed.

I glance at the doctor who was thrown across the room. "Are you okay?"

He utters a high-pitched laugh as he climbs to his feet. Everyone in the room takes a shaky step backward. All of them have eyes locked on my chest, and I glance down. A sigil is burned right through the bandage covering my heart. I recognize it immediately and glance at CJ as I claw at the dressing covering Lucifer's damage, ripping it from my skin.

I stare at the place previously marred by Lucifer's nails, and only Raphael's sigil remains, burned into my skin like a tribal tattoo. The heart monitor registers a strong and steady beat and I'm not sure what to say.

"I guess I should *not* stand outside in an electrical storm," I finally say, and eyes widen before CJ's chuckle rolls over the room and the tension splits into nervous laughter.

Chapter 16

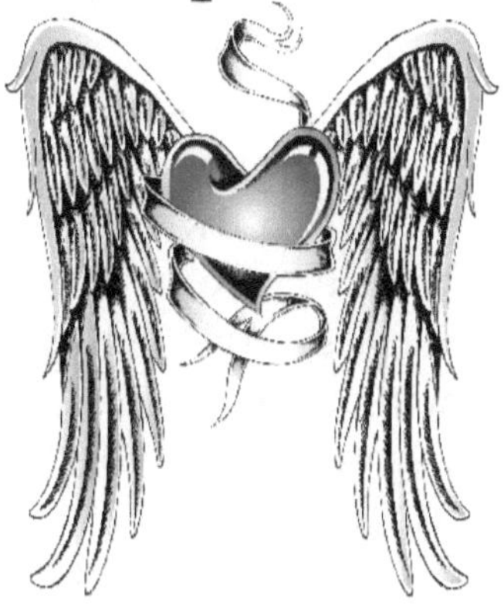

THEY HAVE NO IDEA what the fuck to do with me. I've succumbed to all of their tests after I took a shower and cleaned off any remnants of the horror I endured. Nothing remains of the damage that was there when I was brought in last night.

"We'd like to do more tests," Dr. Wallace says as he flips through my chart.

"No disrespect, but none of your tests is going to provide you with the logical explanation you're looking for." I lean back in the chair and cross my arms. "This one isn't explainable."

"I need to know what happened," he says, pulling his glasses off and pinching the bridge of his nose.

"Divine intervention," I say.

"Bullshit!" He glares at me from across the room.

I lean over and finish lacing my boots. I climb to my feet and grab the duffel bag CJ brought this morning.

"I'm leaving," I say and start out of the room.

"This hospital will not be responsible for any relapse if you leave right now," he snaps.

I glance over my shoulder at him. "I'm pretty sure that's something that will not happen for another forty years or so," I say, and I know it's flippant, but I am tired and hungry and want to eat a fricken moose, and then take a nap in a regular bed, not a hospital cot where they can observe the freak.

I walk outside, expecting CJ, but Bridget leans against her car instead.

"I don't smell like death and coffee anymore," I say and spread my arms out, giving her my signature grin.

Her lips spread into a tight smile and she nods, slipping into the driver's seat without a word. I toss my bag onto the back and then drop into the passenger seat with a huff.

"I need to eat," I say through a yawn.

"I'm sure your brother has something you can grab." The chill in her voice hits and I glance at her.

"You're pissed at me?"

She sends me a sideways glare. "Is this the way it's always going to be?" she snaps the question out.

"I didn't plan on dying, Bridget. It just fucking happened, okay?"

"What exactly happened in there?" Her hands grip the steering wheel so hard her knuckles are white.

I take a deep breath, calming myself. "You didn't get the tune he was whistling?"

She looks at me with a crease between her eyes. "Whistle while you Work from Snow White. Why?"

I just stare at her and cock my head.

She shrugs and looks back at the road. "Well?"

"Take a closer look at those memories of when I was nine." I glance out the side window.

We pass harbor beach and the church while she drifts through the memories. As we approach CJ's road, she gasps and nearly misses the turn. The car bounces off the curb before she gets control of it again and stops before we get to the curve in the road. Throwing the vehicle in park, she turns to me, her eyes wide enough for me to explain.

"It all came back like that." I snap my fingers. "So did the terror, and I guess CJ wasn't kidding about how fragile my heart was."

She quietly digests the new information, chewing on her bottom lip in a way that makes me want to kiss her, but I refrain. When her eyes drift back to mine, she says, "So, if we had taken you home and something triggered you, you would have died?"

I don't answer because she is probably right; instead, I look out the windshield. The electric shock did something, and if I hadn't been in the hospital... my mind doesn't even entertain the 'what if' involved, and I glance at Bridget.

"Technically, I did die." A chill skitters from my neck to my tailbone, and I grimace. "And you screaming at me was the only reason I didn't just fade to black."

She stares at me.

"So, thank you," I add.

She blinks and does a little shake of her head, as if something morbid crawled under her skin, before she focuses back on the road. With a deep breath, she puts the car in drive. "You're welcome," she says, without looking at me. "But it was the defibrillator, not me."

Her mind is swirling so fast that I'm only getting an image here and a thought there, and every memory is heart wrenching.

"It was you. Without your rant, I wouldn't have been trying to get back into my body at the precise moment they shocked me." I chew on the inside of my lip, debating on asking if I should really expect a future with her, especially after the pain I've caused.

She pulls through the broken gate and parks.

I grab her hand before she gets out, and she stops with one foot on the driveway and looks back at me. "What?"

The snap in her voice makes me let her go. "Nothing." I step out of the car and follow her to the door, where she waves for me to lead the way.

I open the door, and stare at the banner hung haphazardly across the living room. Noisemakers and streamers meet me, and if I *had* had a weak heart, the shock of the welcoming party would have put me into cardiac arrest. The words written on the banner pull a grin from me. Welcome back from the dead! I particularly liked the electrified skeleton they hung from one end, like a seriously twisted after-thought.

I meet my brother's gaze and he shrugs, looking over his shoulder at his handiwork, with the same stupid grin I'm sure I'm wearing. I turn on Bridget and point at her.

"You knew about this?"

Her light laugh caresses my soul and without her permission, I pull her against me and plant a serious kiss on her laughing lips.

I let more time pass than appropriate in a room full of onlookers before I break the kiss and step inside.

I stare at the sign and my smile fades. Everyone I truly care about stands in my brother's living room, and for a moment, I feel the loss of those who aren't here celebrating this moment with us. My gaze lands on Naomi and her family, and I give a nod.

Grace is the first person to approach, and she steps forward tentatively.

"Thank you," she says, and I just swallow the lump in my throat.

"I'm sorry your father wasn't here to see this day," I say, in a voice squeezed with emotion.

Her palm cups my cheek. "This was meant to pass," she says, and that age-old wisdom I remember clouds her eyes. "The righteous man has to fall in order to claim the light and banish the darkness." Her hand dropped from my cheek. "I never understood that until now."

"Where did you hear that?" I ask, and she gives me that soft smile that reminds me of both her mother and father at the same moment.

"The angels have been telling me that all my life," she answers, and I can't help but shiver and glance up at Naomi.

I utter a laugh. "So much for chance," I say, and Naomi actually allows a tight smile. She still does not like me, and being in the same room is painful for her.

"They also wanted me to let you know you've earned your salvation. Lucifer is no longer a threat to us, and for that, they are grateful."

I have to bite my lip against the sudden swell of emotion those words bring to the surface, and I give Grace a quick hug before crossing to Naomi.

"I know there isn't a thing I can do to fix what I've done to you and your family…"

She puts her fingers over my mouth. "It had to be you." She looks over my shoulder at Grace and then back at me. "And as much as I hate you for killing my husband, I know it had to be you, and it had to be him." Tears form in her eyes. "It was the only way for us to be free and that's all he ever wanted."

I drop my chin to my chest, fighting the burn in my eyes and at the back of my throat. "I miss him," I whisper, knowing my feelings on the matter are nothing compared to hers. He had been my best friend, my pillar when shit hit the fan, and he never once let me down. Killing him had nearly killed me. I meet her gaze and she rolls her lower lip between her teeth and nods before she pulls me into a hug.

When she releases me, I step back, scanning the room.

"Hey," I say to Paige and Austin. Outside of the small conversation at their house before hell broke loose, we hadn't really had a chance to talk. I was looking forward to getting reacquainted with them once things settled down.

"I guess this is all that is left of the angel bloodlines." Austin says, and I glance around the room.

"Twelve."

"The number of zodiac signs," Paige says with a smile.

I let out a laugh and turn back to Bridget, who stands right next to CJ. My gaze rises to the skeleton again just as another zap hits it. "Nice touch. Whose idea was that?"

The dimples carved in Bridget's cheeks give me the answer even before CJ points at her. I glance at our daughter.

"Your mother is seriously twisted," I say, and she just blushes and glances at Bridget with a nod.

"I have a bottle with your name on it in the other room," CJ says, and he shuffles his feet before he steps through the kitchen entry. The group flows through the door before I can, and I'm not sure if it's coordinated or just coincidence that I am left last with Bridget.

I grab her arm, stopping her from following the rest of the crew.

"So the car?" I hook my thumb over my shoulder. "You weren't really pissed?"

Her smile fades a notch. "CJ's been teaching me how to hide my thoughts, and it seems I'm most successful when I'm angry or hurt, so I just kept replaying those things in my head. And yeah, it still pisses me off that you left and made a conscious choice not to answer any of my calls, so I used it."

"Well, you did a great job. And that," I look up again at the extra special twist in the sign. "Is fucking fantastic," I add with a grin.

She takes my hand and leads me into the back room where everyone has gathered. I cross to the sliders and CJ hands me a glass of Dewars. I glance at the lawn and CJ wasn't kidding. It was a mess, with spots of black patches mixed with rust patches. "Did you try holy water?" I ask, nodding at the black mess.

CJ and Valerie exchange a glance and both of them shake their head.

"Neither of us even thought of that," Valerie laughs.

I offer my best 'maybe you should try' smile and focus back on the yard.

"We have hot dogs and hamburgers along with macaroni and cheese for everyone tonight," CJ says. "It's time to celebrate."

"Celebrating sounds great!" I say, and I'm not sure I mean it, but I sip my scotch and take a seat on the couch, observing the family dynamics I had missed for the last ten years. After a flurry of activity in the kitchen, the kids run downstairs with arms full of snacks and soda. CJ and Austin chat over by the refrigerator, while the women work as a team in the kitchen, putting together snacks for us.

Bridget catches me watching out of the corner of her eye and stops, turning towards me, and she just leans on the counter with a smile. I had her memories. I should know how close she has gotten to my family, but seeing it in action leaves an emptiness in my center, along with a sliver of envy. I raise my glass at her and down the scotch.

The warm flow spreads through me, and I close my eyes. The couch cushion shifts and I open my eyes, taking in Bridget's beautiful hazel eyes.

"Are you okay?" she asks softly, studying me, looking for any sign of weakness that might indicate a relapse of some sort.

"I'm fine." I look at the group continuing to talk and work together. "I just haven't been in a lot of social situations in quite a few years." When my gaze returned to hers, I press my lips together in a slight smile. "I'm not good at small talk."

"Since when?"

I laugh. "Since always."

"You used to be the center of attention," she says.

"That's only because people had to watch my hands to know what the hell I was saying." I chuckle, looking at her sideways.

"Yeah, well, your hands were magic," she mumbles and goes to stand up.

"What?"

She smiles. "All the girls watched your hands because we wanted them on us, and all the guys watched because your hands could catch a rocket at fifty yards."

"And here I thought it was because I had such interesting things to say."

"About what?" CJ says, and takes a seat on the other couch, looking between us.

"I was just teasing your brother," Bridget says, and wanders towards the kitchen and the cheese and cracker spread on the breakfast bar.

CJ watches her go and glances at me, tilting his head in her direction.

"I don't need dating advice from you," I say and lean forward, pouring another glass of scotch. "Besides, there's no rush. We'll eventually figure it out." I follow his gaze, and her light laugh drifts over the room.

The rest of the night passes in surreal slow motion. Laughter prevails, and it isn't the sarcastic or tension filled laughter of the last fifteen years. It's strange, and a part of me is uncomfortable with it, as if I am going to wake to find our peace is all an illusion.

Naomi has the same haunting in her eyes that I'm experiencing. She's been on the run a hell of a lot longer than any of us, so this has to be just as unnerving to her. She looks up from her conversation, meeting my gaze as if she can read my mind, and I send her a nod along with a closed-lip smile before I finish my drink.

"Did you ever think we'd see this day?" Valerie asks as she steps by my side, scanning the room with me.

"Honestly, no. I'm still waiting for the bomb to drop."

"I think we all are," she says and drapes her arm over my shoulder. "But for now, I say we seize the day!" Her grin is infections and I clink my empty glass against hers in a show of solidarity.

Chapter 17

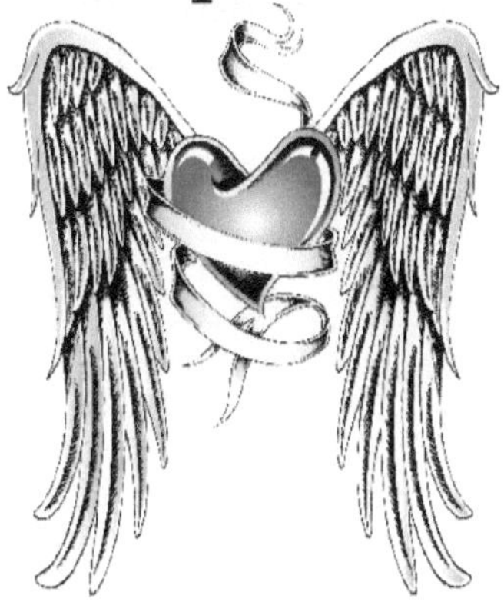

SUNSHINE WAKES ME AND I cover my eyes with my arm, but it's enough to get my mind moving, even though it's sluggish from alcohol consumption. I roll onto my side, even though I know it's useless. Once my brain shifts into gear, there is no more sleep coming until the most inopportune moment of the day.

After a shower and a change of clothes, I climb down the stairs and fix myself a cup of coffee, retreating outside in the cool morning sunshine. I find my perch on the rock wall and stare out at the water. Movement pulls my attention back towards the house and Naomi is a few feet away.

"Morning," I say and she takes a seat.

"Morning," she glances out over the water and turns towards me. "This is all too weird."

A low laugh comes from deep within my chest. "Very." My gaze drifts towards the damaged lawn. "I didn't expect to live," I say and meet her gaze.

"Neither did I," she says softly. "I guess now that this is all over, I should think about trying to move on."

I give her a slow nod. "Just don't let anyone take advantage of you."

Her curt laugh draws a smile and heat rises in my cheeks.

"You know what I mean," I say and roll my eyes. "Just out of curiosity, is there anyone in particular?"

Now it is her turn to blush, and she moves her hand back and forth.

I raise an eyebrow.

"One of the teachers at the high school has shown interest," she mumbles, and sips her coffee. "But he's a lot younger than I am."

"Look at you, going all cougar and shit," I say, grinning, and the look she sends me should have shut me up right there, but I've never been good with keeping my thoughts to myself since my wife's tongue replaced mine. "So, have you... um, sampled the goods?"

"Oh. My. God." She stands up and walks away.

"Naomi?" I ask, stopping her and she looks over her shoulder at me. "Damian wouldn't want you to be alone for the rest of your life."

She keeps her back to me. "I couldn't bring anyone into this nightmare."

I sigh, knowing exactly what she meant. "I ran from Bridget for the same reason."

She looks over her shoulder at me and her eyes sparkle as her lips twitch into a smile. "I think it's time we both sampled the goods."

I grin and sip my coffee as she wanders back to her house, laughing under her breath. The sea lulls me into thought, and they turn to Bridget, as they have since I drove away ten years ago. I glance at my watch. The bus has already come and gone, if my memory serves me and I head inside, retrieving the small box that I carried back from Greece.

"I'm borrowing the truck," I say aloud to the quiet house.

Okay, CJ's sleepy voice echoes in my head, and I grab the keys off the peg. The drive is short, and I sit in the cab, staring at the house, wondering exactly what I'm going to say. I can't exactly walk in the door and just blurt out the question on my mind.

I continue to stare at the house, inspecting my intentions a little closer, and then I slip out of the car and stroll to the door, looping the keys around my finger to settle the nerves biting at me.

I poise my hand to knock and then drop it, turning away. Staring at the river across the way, I can't help but wonder if Bridget is better off without me. I close my eyes and turn back to the door with my hands on my hips.

Now that the danger isn't lurking anymore, will she still see someone worthy of her love, or have I screwed this up so much that she'll finally see under the facade?

I grit my teeth and knock on the door.

The faint shuffle of feet on the wood floor drifts through the door, and when the wood door swings open, I offer an uncomfortable smile.

"Hi." I stare at her and lick my lips, unsure of what else to say. My eyes flow down the blue silk shirt to the cream skirt and the sexy open-toed heels. She makes me feel grossly underdressed in my jeans and flannel shirt.

"You don't need to knock. This is your business, too." She points up in the air and my gaze follows to the sign still carrying my name, while Bridget swings the door open for me.

"But you and April live here, and I don't want to impose." I know I'm reaching, but I can't figure out what her deal is today.

"Tom, you own the business and this house." She rolls her eyes at me when I step inside.

Technically, she's right. If I wanted to be a dick, I could insist on living here and she would have no choice, but I'm not. Nor do I want to be.

"Since you're back..." she hands me a stack of call transcripts and turns, heading into the only office left. I stare after her, and a low simmer burns at the sexy sway of her hips before she sashays out of sight. My gaze drops to the notes. I shuffle through them as I cross into Damian's old office.

I stop in the door and blink at the brightness before me. The only familiar item is the desk, and she slides into the comfortable looking ergonomic chair, turning towards the computer monitor. The rest of the decor has changed drastically from my old partner's dark tastes.

Now this space is light, almost too light, in my opinion. Even the furniture radiates a sunny disposition, which is in direct contrast to Bridget right now. She is all business, and I take one more scan, looking for an alternate workstation as if it would materialize out of nowhere.

"Where am I supposed to work?" I ask, and she looks up from the computer, nodding towards the couches.

"You can set up over there until we can get another desk." She turns her focus back to the computer.

Her lack of warmth has me a little confused, especially after the heat I felt from her yesterday when I kissed her at the house. I step closer to the desk. "Bri?"

Her hands pause over the keys, and she takes a deep breath before facing me and folding her arms on the desk. When she tilts her head and purses her lips, I'm not sure what to say.

It's been a long time since I felt like a scolded kid, but that's the vibe I am getting right now. I can't read a thing from her, which is more than frustrating.

I drop the pile of notes on the desk, meeting her hard and inquisitive gaze.

"I'm working, Tom," she says, and even her tone is terse.

That old familiar frustrated burn fills my stomach and I walk around the side of the desk. She swivels the chair, so she is facing me and crosses her arms. I lean forward, planting a hand on each chair arm, staring her down.

"You are right. This is my business, so stop treating me like I'm a junior intern on my first day."

The edges of her lips twitch.

"So, what exactly are you going to do to me, boss man?" Her voice fills with spitfire, but her cheeks flush in response to my close proximity.

My gaze drifts from her eyes to her now slightly parted lips, and then drops to the opening of her silk shirt, giving me a peek at her cleavage. I take a chance.

"What exactly would you have me do?" I ask in an equally terse tone.

A dimple appears before she locks it down, but the sparkle in her eyes tells me what I need to know. When she doesn't answer, I slowly drop to my knees.

"Would you have me beg for your forgiveness?" I ask, letting my hands drop to the side of the chair, my thumbs just barely grazing the outside of her silk-clad thighs.

"That's a start," she says.

"Perhaps instead of begging, I need to earn it." My hands move onto her thighs, drifting down to her knees before gradually moving upwards under the skirt. Her skin quivers under my touch.

"Perhaps." Her voice falls into that husky quality I remember from my dreams, and I stop.

The flare of wanting in her eyes resumes my momentum and I close in, meeting her parted lips with mine, just as my fingers graze her bare pussy. I chuckle against her lips.

"You are so very... naughty," I whisper and deepen the kiss, remembering the dream and the reality of her all at once. This time I do pause, and pull away from her mouth. Our eyes lock. My hand still plays with her and her thighs part, inviting me to do more than just caress her.

Heat fills my cheeks and I let out a laugh. "I don't have anything."

She smiles and opens the desk drawer, lifting out a strip of condoms.

"When did you pick those up?" I ask, hoping it wasn't some random time between when I left and today, but her answer just makes my heart pound faster in my chest.

"Last night on the way home," she says and tears one off; dropping it on the desk so I don't have to interrupt the slow stroke between her legs.

I stop long enough to push the silk up her thighs and then pull her to the edge of the seat. I'm in no hurry, and I do want to hear her beg for me until she's so wet she can't speak. I tease her, running my tongue slowly up the inside of her thigh before repeating on her other leg.

Her hand fists in my hair when my tongue rolls around her sensitive clit.

"Jesus, Tom," she whispers. "Just... just don't stop,"

I move away, sucking her thigh before returning to where she wants me. There is no level of control that can keep me from doing as she bids and I give in. She cries out under the manipulation of my tongue. Ten years of pent-up sexual frustration rushes out of her in waves and my build up is just as acute.

She whimpers in the chair. Her hands grasp my hair as if this is a dream she doesn't want to let go. The absolute rhapsody painted on her face makes me smile, and the salty-sweet taste of her drives me wild. My entire body pulses with the need building inside me and I pull away, climbing to my feet and fumbling with my belt. My breath matches hers, raspy and ragged, and she moves my hands away, unzipping my jeans and pulling my hard member out.

I squeeze my eyes closed, trying to hold on, but the moment her mouth wraps around the tip of my cock, I lose it.

"Oh, fuck." My whisper is enclosed in an exhale, and Bridget sucks with each spurt, stroking me with both her mouth and her hand. I finally pull away and lean against the desk, tucking my junk back into my underwear.

I open my eyes with a sigh, meeting Bridget's gaze. "Just give me a few minutes and then we can start over again."

She grins and stands up, placing her palm on the front of my pants, stroking.

I stare into her eyes and tuck a strand of hair behind her ears before I pull her into a gentle kiss. Just the friction of her hand against my underwear starts my revival and I pull away.

"I want more," I say and she smiles, misinterpreting my statement.

"In a few minutes, you'll get your wish," she purrs and leans in, kissing my neck.

"No, Bridget. I'm not talking about sex. I want more than just this."

She slowly pulls away and her eyes lock on mine as her hand slows.

"I want to wake with you by my side." I let out a laugh. "I want to continue sharing everything going on inside my head and my heart with you. I want to experience your joys and your fears firsthand, instead of through your memories, and I want to be a father to my daughter."

"How about we start out dating?" She interrupts me.

I raise my eyebrows. "You want me to wine and dine you?"

She blushes. "It would be kind of a nice change," she says.

"I guess I can do that," I say and bite my lip. Her hand is still pressed against me. "But I want to do it while under the same roof."

"Mmmm," she says and shakes her head. "That might send the wrong message."

"Really?" I lean away from her. "We can fuck until the cows come home, but the minute I hang my hat on the door, *THAT* sends the wrong message?"

Her eyes narrow and she pulls her hand away, crossing her arms. "You think you can just waltz back into my life and decide you want to shack up?"

"You're the one who wants to start with just dating," I say, using finger quotes around the words just dating, before I cross my arms. Whatever heat had been building between us was now as cool as the arctic.

I turn and pick up the unopened condom. "Am I just a good fuck to you?" I toss it at her and button my pants, escaping while I still have some dignity left.

"No. Tom, you know damned well you mean more to me," she snaps before I get to the door, and I stop.

"So, what is it you want? What does our future look like to you?"

Silence blankets us long enough for me to look over my shoulder.

"Everything we've done, we've done during a crisis. I don't know what we will be like without that," she says. "And if for some reason it doesn't work between us... I can't do that to April."

"Then what was all this about?" I turn and wave at the desk.

She raises her shoulders and they fall in defeat.

I'm not sure whether to stay or go.

"I stood outside for a good ten minutes before I knocked." I say, looking at the ceiling. "Because I wanted to make sure I was here for the right reasons." I drop my gaze to hers. "And not just because you are one of the sexiest women I know." I shift, uncomfortable with baring my soul with words. "I wanted to make sure that all that time away didn't make this more than it really was."

Her gaze bounces from my hands to my face and she sighs.

My hands are signing out of habit, even after this long, I fall into the same pattern when I'm out of my element. I let out a nervous chuckle. "I still sign when I'm nervous." I shove my hands into my pockets.

"Why are you nervous?" she asks.

"Because I feel like I've already lost you."

Bridget slowly lowers into the chair, studying me. "I'm scared," she admits, almost too softly for me to pick up, but the words echo in my head, melting my nerves.

"Why?"

"I can't handle another loss," she says, and the tears shining in her eyes squeeze my heart.

"Neither can I," I say. "But here's the thing. I can't walk away, either." I cross to the desk, and pull a small package out of my pocket and set it down on the wood between us. "You asked if there was anything I was hiding from you in my memories?" I point to the box. "I lied when I said no. I hid that."

Bridget's eyebrows rise, and she stares at the box before her gaze moves up to mine. "When did you get that?" she asks without reaching for the offering.

"I bought it in Greece before I came home, and I was hoping like hell I wasn't too late." I let out a nervous laugh. "That was before I found out Lucifer was still topside."

She leans back in the chair, staring at the tiny jewelry box, and my stomach flutters.

"Aren't you going to open it?"

She moves her gaze up to mine. "There's a part of me that is still pissed at you."

I reach for the box, intending to pocket it again, but she moves faster, covering it with her hand. The gesture is enough to inform me we are not done yet, but she doesn't pick it up. Instead, she moves it a little closer before taking a deep breath.

"How do you know you won't tire of me, or worse, get bored?"

"I highly doubt either of those things will ever happen."

"But how do you know?"

I lean my hip on the desk and study her chaotic aura. "Because you can still drive me bat shit crazy," I say, focusing on her in the center of the rainbow of contrasting colors. Her cheeks bloom red. "I'm not talking about our bedroom compatibility, Bri. Although, admittedly, if that had sucked, neither of us would be here right now."

"No pun intended?"

I grin and look down at my hands. "No, no pun intended." I close my eyes for a minute, calming the energy in my core. "If you want to date, that's what we'll do." I open my eyes, trying to squash the growing disappointment. "We have time."

"If I hadn't been such a bitch when you came in, what would have happened?"

I debate, and before I lose my nerve, I swipe the box from the desk and step around the corner in front of her. With my heart pounding in my throat, I drop to my knee and flip open the box.

"Marry me, Bridget."

She stares at me with her jaw hanging open. Her eyes never fall to the box or the engagement ring inside. There is a big nothingness in her mind, as if my actions short-circuited her.

I snap the box closed and stand up. "But you'd just like to date, so..." I turn around and she's on her feet, grabbing my arm and trying to turn me towards her.

"You really aren't kidding," she says with wide eyes.

"No, I'm serious. I'll date you if that's what you want," I say, trying not to let a smile surface.

"Was that a serious proposal?" Her voice rises to a near hysterical pitch, and panic of a lost chance flares in her eyes and her mind. She steps in front of me. "Tom?" she asks when I don't answer.

I open the box and hold it up within her line of vision. Finally, her gaze moves from me to the ring. Her hand flutters over her mouth as she stares at the white and black diamonds intertwined on the band and the sparkling one-carat rock in the center.

"Does that look like I'm kidding?" I say softly, especially since her eyes look as if they might pop out of her head at any second. "I want to make love to you every night, and then make you pancakes in the morning. I want to take you dancing, and to see a play on opening night in New York. I want to take you to Paris and Ireland, and anywhere else you want to go, just to see those places through your eyes. I want to be there with you through whatever kind of shit we get stuck in, and I'm sure we will see our fair share, but with you standing next to me, we can brave any storm they send at us. So, yes. I'm serious. I want to marry you. All you have to do is say yes."

She cocks her head. "Pancakes?"

"I make a mean stack of pancakes," I say with a smile. "So, can I take that as a yes?"

She looks at the ring and then back into my eyes and the slow smile spreading on her lips is my answer. If we needed some sign that this was right, it is delivered the moment I slide the ring on her finger. It fits perfectly.

Framing her face with my palms, I deliver a kiss that sears my soul to hers and she melts into me, lighting some of my more basic needs. We move this to the couch, and as she climbs onto my lap, I can't help but believe redemption exists and she's the catalyst.

"I love you, Thomas Patrick Ryan," she says, before she crushes my response with her lips.

The End

Continue with CJ and Tom's story in Hunting the Siren, the third book in The Paradox files.

About J.E. Taylor

J.E. Taylor is a USA Today bestselling author, a publisher, an editor, a manuscript formatter, a mother, a wife, a business analyst, and a Supernatural fangirl. Not necessarily in that order. She first sat down to seriously write in February of 2007 after her daughter asked:

"Mom, if you could do anything, what would you do?"

From that moment on, she hasn't looked back.

Besides being co-owner of Novel Concept Publishing, Ms. Taylor also moonlights as a Senior Editor of Allegory E-zine, an online venue for Science Fiction, Fantasy and Horror, and co-host of the popular YouTube talk show Spilling Ink.

She lives in New Hampshire with her husband and during the summer months enjoys her weekends on the shore in southern Maine.

Visit her at www.jetaylor75.com to check out her other titles.

If you liked ANGEL FURY, check out the rest of
THE RYAN CHRONICLES:

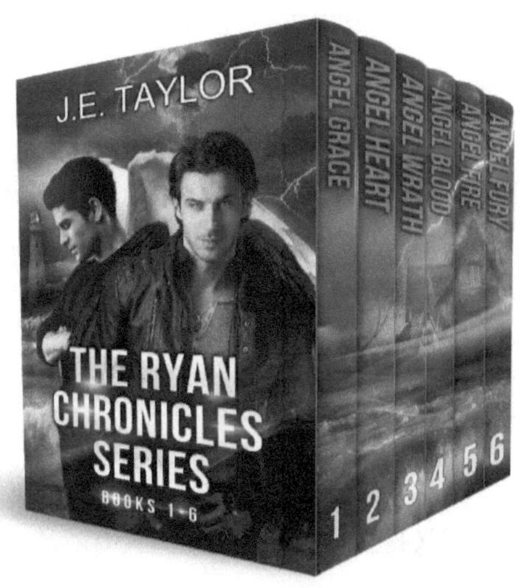

THE RYAN CHRONICLES

**Demons, vampires, angels, and the devil.
What the hell kind of nightmare do I live in?**

CJ Ryan was born with enough psychic power to
destroy the earth. And Lucifer wants him to do just
that.

Raised with a strong moral compass, CJ won't
sacrifice innocent lives to protect his own, and that
puts him at odds with the devil.

But if he doesn't give in, he and all he loves will
become the target of Lucifer's rage.

When CJ gives his twin brother, Tom, a dose of his
powers to keep him safe, it puts Tom directly in
Lucifer's crosshairs.

195

As the final battle draws near, what will they have to sacrifice to keep their loved ones safe?

Can they survive the devil's wrath?

THE RYAN CHRONICLES includes these titles:

CJ's Story:

ANGEL GRACE - Book 1

ANGEL HEART - Book 2

ANGEL WRATH – Book 3

Tom's Story:

ANGEL BLOOD - Book 4

ANGEL FIRE - Book 5

ANGEL FURY – Book 6

Fans of Supernatural and Shadowhunters will enjoy this series.

You might also like the GAMES THRILLER SERIES which highlights CJ and Tom's parents and their unorthodox history together.

GAMES THRILLER SERIES

Intensely disturbing. Beautifully horrific. Indescribably intense.

When Ty Aris kidnaps Jessica Connor for his stepbrother's underground film network, he is not prepared for the impact she has on him.

His obsession with her lights a fire under his ass to get out of the ungodly business with his stepbrother.

But the only way to leave the business is in a body bag.

In the dark plane between life and death, Ty is given a choice: save his soulmate or save his very soul.

The Games Thriller Series includes:

Fallen – A Games Series Prequel

Survival Games

Mind Games

End Game

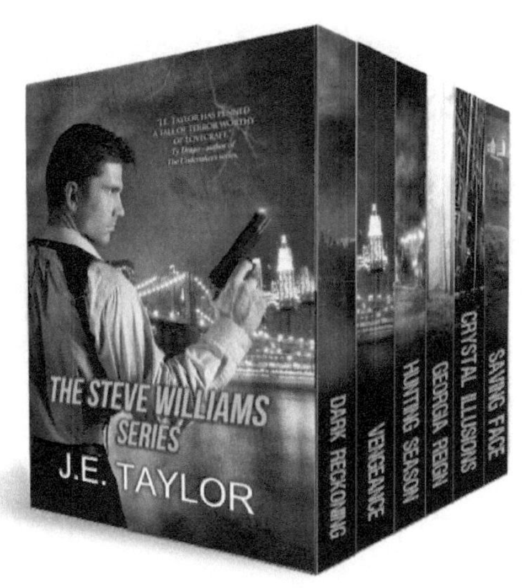

THE STEVE WILLIAMS SERIES

Special Agent Steve Williams excels at his job, catching the most heinous of monsters walking the earth.

Serial killers.

When his job brings him face to face with a psychic, he struggles to accept her gifts in his neat little black and white world. Armed with her visions, along with his skills as an FBI agent, he hunts the worst of the worst, but will he catch the killer before they set their sights on him?

Unstoppable, breath stealing, and terrifying all at once.

Gripping, rich and magnificent!

The Steve Williams Series mixes compelling crime thrillers with supernatural forces that will grip the reader from page one. This six-book series takes you through some of Steve Williams' darkest cases in his FBI career.

The STEVE WILLIAMS SERIES includes Dark Reckoning, Vengeance, Hunting Season, Georgia Reign, Crystal Illusions, and Saving Face.

Find these titles and other fantasy and suspense titles on J.E. Taylor's website!

www.JETaylor75.com